Love
Don & Deb

THE GUNBEARERS

There were three of them, Matt Hendry, Zack Harmon and George Beaudry. They had never been anything but rangemen, and now, finally, in an act of rebellion against Fate, they teamed up to plunder a countryside.

They did it too. But they neglected to consider the capability of the Town Marshal of Almarjal township, Thad Mercer.

He led the final manhunt which nailed all three of them, and a very short career as outlaws came to an end in a blaze of gunfire in a high-country mountain meadow.

The Gunbearers

by

HARRY FOSTER

ST. MARTIN'S PRESS
NEW YORK

ROBERT HALE LIMITED
LONDON

© *Robert Hale Limited 1979*
First published in Great Britain 1979

ISBN 0 7091 7277 X (*Large print edition*)
ISBN 0 7091 7286 9 (*Standard edition*)

Robert Hale Limited
Clerkenwell House
Clerkenwell Green
London, EC1R 0HT

St. Martin's Press Inc.
175 Fifth Avenue
New York, N.Y. 10010

ISBN–0–312–35342–1 (*Standard Edition*)
ISBN–0–312–35343–X (*Large Print Edition*)

Library of Congress Catalog Card Number 78–65942

Printed in Great Britain
by Billing & Sons Limited, Guildford, London and Worcester

1

NEW MEXICO

He broke his leg turning a stampede in the brake-country of Nebraska and one of the advantages of working for a large cow outfit was that it worked no noticeable hardship to have an invalid around throughout the riding season.

The horse had gone down at a dead run, pitching George Beaudry pinwheel-like to land with his left leg curled under him. When he recovered consciousness the camp-cook had doused him with stinging liniment in the open cuts and scrapes and scratches until he burnt in so many places he did not for a few moments realise they had yanked his leg out straight and had splinted and bandaged it that way. In fact the leg hurt a lot less than the cuts and bruises.

When he had looked up the *cosinero* was leering from an unshaven face, showing teeth yellowed by half a century of chewing Kentucky twist. The cook had said, "I've seen fellers hurt worse'n this and they never even stopped talking," then he cackled.

Behind him had been standing Matthew Hendry and Zachary Harman who had hired on the same day as George Beaudry and who, like George, had been learning methods, boundaries and procedures ever since. They had become friends, mostly out of necessity. They were the only newcomers at the camps, and down at the bunkhouse. All the other hands had been riding for the outfit every season for a number of years and they had pretty much of a closed fraternity. Sometimes, on the big outfits it worked out that way.

Later, when George had been able to hobble about on home-made crutches, some of the older hands made little remarks ... "Sure beats hell out of workin' for your keep, don't it?" and now and then something like, "Wisht'ell I was smart enough to bust a leg first week of the season and get paid for lyin' 'round all the rest of the summer—and get fed to-boot."

Once, when George dug out his Colt and buckled the shellbelt on, Matt Hendry had come into the bunkhouse doorway, had looked, then had wagged his head wearing his customary good-natured smile.

"Forget it," he had admonished. "You got to expect 'em to feel that way, George. I sort of envy you myself, when it's raining like a big cow peein' on a flat rock and I got to be out in it while you're in here next to the stove and all ... You put on that damned gun and they'll gang up on you and never let you have a decent moment. Take it off, George. You just got to take their ragging is all."

It was good sound advice and George had indeed shoved the coiled belt and Colt back into his warbag.

Once, when he was learning to navigate on the crutches a man named Clay Bourne, a dark man with the high, flat cheekbones of a 'breed, playfully roped one of the crutches from the bunkhouse porch.

But that did not come off so well. The rangeboss, a hard, taciturn man with a knife-scarred chin had turned and said, "You think that's funny? What would you think if I kicked half the gawddamned wadding out of you?"

It had been a long summer. The longest one in the life of George Beaudry. He mended harness, hobbled around tending branding-fires, tried his utmost, and cursed the dragging stiffness of the splinted leg until most of the men came round to a grudging acceptance of his exasperation and now and then would even gruffly sympathise a little.

There was a lot of time to think, to speculate about things, to take stock, to remember earlier times, even to make a few plans although ordinarily George Beaudry was typical of his profession—he never planned beyond tomorrow. Hadn't, that is, up until he'd had all summer to hobble around by himself and do a little stock-taking.

Autumn arrived a little early that year. At least in Nebraska it did, so the big outfits made an early gather and got ready to drive either overland to a market or down-country somewhere to rails-end.

It was cold work and hard, with nights in the saddle and windy days when the cold went right on through everything a man could button on to himself.

George could ride. Not far and not with much comfort yet, but he could straddle his private horse when it came time to pick up his final wages. He and Zack Harmon and Matt Hendry. The other two had decided between themselves not to stay on during the drive.

The leathery old hands had sneered. There were

riders in the crew who at forty were still proving their manhood each time a challenge came up. There were men like that in every riding crew, in just about every country. Most of them would go right on proving their toughness right up to the day they would die. It went with the profession.

But when George and Matt and Zack rode off the ranch and down to Spearhead to buy a sack of supplies, have a few straight-shots at the saloon, then head on out, there was not one shred of shame or remorse among them.

It wasn't that any one of the three of them could not have matched those older men. They could have, hands down. It was rather that they did not choose to, and there was no law which said they had to, so as they headed south-westerly from Spearhead it was in the general direction of warmer country.

"New Mexico," stated George, his bad leg being allowed to hang free on the left side, rather than being compelled to follow the round warp of the horse, "that's where the sunshine spends the winter. And there's work, if a feller is among the first ones to get down there."

The other two listened. They were north-western rangemen. Even Nebraska had seemed a long way south to them. None of the three of them had been working the ranges a lot of years. Matthew Hendry was the eldest he had just barely reached his thirties. But they were lean and sinewy young men whose countenances had been exposed to all kinds of weather over the past few years. They did not look especially young; not old either but not as young as they were, and over the weeks after they rode out of

Spearhead since they had no reason to shave often, they didn't, and also because as free men, unhindered by any ties as well as being uninhibited, they took their time, meandered off the trail when they felt like it and, except for an occasional glance over their shoulders to test the wind and to study autumn skies, they made no attempt to hurry.

Twice they were driven into towns by thunderstorms. Both times they pulled out the moment the sun returned even though the ground was treacherous underfoot.

Only once, and that was after they'd ridden out of Springfield in Colorado bound west to Trinidad, then down through the high pass into Raton, New Mexico, did they seriously discuss what they were doing down there. Zack and Matt were by this time accustomed to pleasantly riding through fresh lands. It was easy to adjust to a camping, foot-loose, roaming variety of existence, but when they were atop the high pass gazing down across the heat-blued far distances of New Mexico, George said, "I grew up down here. I first got bucked off a horse and chased by an old wet-cow down here. First time I ever saw a rich man, or a Texan, was down here." He looked around and laughed. "First lady I ever touched with both hands at the same time was down there too."

Zack said, "Well hell; if New Messico's got all that—*and* sunshine, what we settin' up atop these rocks for?"

They angled down through the high pass by picking their way around the long- spending slope using a trail as old as the territory itself, and once when their horses picked up bear-scent they had to dismount and wait, otherwise the terrified beasts might have gone straight down and it was an awful long way to the bottom of the pass. Later, when dusk was close, they found a place with a blackened old stone-ring for a supper fire where generations of men, red and brown as well as white, had chosen to camp for two excellent reasons. There was a little creek close at hand, and anyone squatting up there could sweep the area in all directions without being in danger of a bushwhack.

George told them of the Indians, Comanches but mostly the Apaches, who had at one time owned this entire area and had pushed the boundaries of Mexico back five hundred miles, and had kept them back there. He produced a bottle of whisky from his bedroll, which his companions stared at since none of them had been near a town in quite a while, and as he prised out the cork and handed it around, he said, "Something I want to tell you fellers. South of here, below Raton and on out of Lincoln County where I grew up, there's a place called Almarjal. It's a Mex word—you say it like this: Al-mar-hal. You understand? It means a sort of meadow where cattle graze."

Zack was interested. "Messicans sure can crowd a heap of meaning into one word. Al-mar-hal." He nodded as though satisfied with his mastery of the pronunciation. Then he said, "Rode with a feller two summers back in the Lodgepole country of Montana who'd rode down here a season or two, and he said just about everything's got a Mex name."

"The territory used to belong to them," stated George. "When we taken it over, well, folks just kept the Mex names. Except some, and they was just too damned hard to say." He accepted the bottle from Matt, tipped back his head, swallowed several times, then swore and coughed at the same time, dashed water from his eyes with a soiled sleeve and drove the cork fiercely back down into the bottle. "Gawddamn but that's awful tastin' stuff," he rasped, and set the bottle aside. "Getting back ... There's something I want to tell you fellers.

"I grew up in Almarjal. I told you that. It's rich cow country, and they got some big outfits down there—and money. Some pretty well-off cowmen, and money in the bank as well as cattle out over one hell of a big area. And the town—it may look Mex with adobe buildings and all, but it's American through and through ... Well; at least the business part of it and most of the residential part of it, but there's a place called Mex-town and that out back of town; that's the old part."

"Messicans live back there?" asked Zack.

"Yes."

"Ain't allowed to live with the whites?"

George had to stop and think a moment. Something people had taken for granted all their lives could rarely ever be explained in one breath, when its roots were deep in divergent cultures and philosophies. "Well," he eventually said, handing Matt the corked bottle again, "I don't think it's that they *can't*, because there was Messicans lived over in our part of town when I was a kid. But they had to own a store or something—have money, you understand. Anyway, most of 'em prefer to live in Old Town—which we always called Mex-town." George watched Matt pass the bottle to Zack Harmon, and frowned as he also said, "Gawddammit, I don't know why a lot of things is as they are. And what I got to tell you about Almarjal don't have much to do with the Messicans. It don't even have a hell of a lot to do with the *gringos*—the whites like us."

Matt rolled a smoke to help dilute the greeny taste of that acidy whisky. As he leaned and lit up, then blew smoke, he looked at George with cheeks which were getting a little redder and eyes which were becoming more bright and shiny by the moment.

"Just what in hell *are* you telling us?" he demanded. "We know you grew up down there. You been sayin' that ever since we left Nebraska. What else is it you got to say about that place? You figure we could get work, and winter in the sun down there?"

George took back the bottle from Zack, considered it balefully for a moment, then tipped it again, and this time he was able to blink away the rush of tears. Nor did he hack and cough and rasp as he'd done before. He too, was getting a little drunk.

He carefully replaced the cork and with equal care laid the nearly empty bottle back away from the fire where his bedroll was. Then he said, "I don't figure we're going to go to work down there. Not on a gawddamned cow ranch anyway. I figure we're going to get rich out of that stinkin' town. Richer'n you fellers got any notion."

Matt continued to sceptically stare but Zack was already turning to punch his blankets around the way he wanted them. He had of course heard George but he was beginning to care less and less about a whole lot of things and talk was one of them.

George leaned and gave Zack a light slap. "Listen," he ordered. "Now just set there and listen. I know that town like I know the back of my hand. I know everyone around down there who's got money. And back in Nebraska I had all summer to think, to figure this out, to plan it so's the three of us are going to come out of Almarjal loaded down with saddlebags full of money." He looked around. "You fellers listening?"

Zack responded instantly. "Hell yes, I'm listening," but Matt said nothing, he simply squatted across the little fire staring, until George caught the strange expression highlighted by their campfire, and said, "Matt ... ?"

The older rangerider was cautious. "Spit it out first, George, then I'll tell you what I think."

"We are going to clean out that town, the bank, the big cowmen, the rich merchants," stated George, challenging Matt with his shiny and bleak look. "I been all summer perfectin' how we're going to do it."

"And get killed by the lousy law," spat out Matt.

George craftily smiled. "Not by a damned sight. We aren't even goin' to run afoul of the law. I told you, damn it all, I been all summer perfectin' this. Matt, you going along or aren't you?"

"I haven't heard enough yet to make up my mind," said the older cowboy.

"Then you just set there and listen," exclaimed George, as he began his slow-spoken hour-long explanation with the night closing in on all sides of them, and with their little cooking-fire gradually dying down almost to coals before Zack roused himself and pitched on some more twigs, then hunched forward to continue listening.

When George finished he and Matt steadily stared at each other before the older rangeman finally said, "All right. All right, I expect a man might as well *be* a damned outlaw as live like one, around campfires like this, and never have any money or much of anything else." Matt turned. "Zack?"

"I guess," murmured the hunched-over man, hugging his knees and gently swaying. "Damned whisky—I can't think straight right now, but I guess it'll work, won't it Matt?"

The elder man sighed and leaned back. "If it does—George's right, we'll be rich. If it don't work ..." Matt shrugged wide, rawboned shoulders. "We'll have to ride like hell."

George felt around behind him for the bottle, pulled the cork, squinted at the meagre contents, then passed it around again.

2

A SUCCESSFUL VISITATION

Thad Mercer had been local lawman in the Almarjal country for almost twelve years, and he had not looked very young when he'd hired on—had been as grey then as he was now—so he really did not look any older twelve years later. He was, people would have said if they'd had occasion to dwell upon it, in the 'prime of his life' which meant that he could have been somewhere between thirty-five and forty-five. Rangemen, it seemed, did not age at all for that one decade out of their lives.

Or if they did age, for most of them it was nothing noticeable. Nor did most rangemen think of themselves in terms of years. They considered their lives in terms of summers, winters, aches and pains.

Thad Mercer had been a rangerider for the first ten years of his working life. He had in fact been a very good rangeman—a tophand. Then he had turned to law enforcement and had been with it ever since.

There certainly were advantages. He never got called out in a blinding, sleety rainstorm to help turn back running cattle, and for the most part during New Mexico's blazing summers he could stay in shade if he really worked at it.

As a lawman he had encountered them all at one time or another—highwaymen, hired bushwhackers, cattle rustlers and horsethieves, claim jumpers, Mex raiders from below the border, bank-robbers and troublesome rangemen who, usually of a Saturday night, took on too big a liquid load and went up and down the roadway with their spurs down a notch and their tie-downs hanging loose, courting trouble.

As he'd once told Blaine Harper who headed up the Stockman's Trust & Savings Bank, in Almarjal, a law officer's work was seventy-five per cent being visible and looking mean enough, and twenty-five per cent being on hand and *being* mean enough.

John Billings, one of the biggest and richest cowmen in the Almarjal countryside, had often warned his seasonal riders not to cross Constable Mercer, because even if they could whip him or maybe outdraw him, that would only be their first error in judgement. Their second error would be on the trail first thing in the morning—a whole passel of townsmen and rangemen—with a hangrope. People, old Billings said plainly enough for everyone to understand, simply did not tolerate unnecessary violence around Almarjal, and they would pursue troublemakers the same as they'd go after outlaws— meting out an identical variety of justice to both.

It was sound advice. Coming from a man who hired more riders than any of the other cowmen around, it carried a lot of weight. But Blaine Harper and Old Man Billings were far from being alone in their firm conviction that law and order were paramount. The entire community, in fact the entire Almarjal countryside, was unshakable in its belief that unless folks had law, and maintained order, not only would their lives as well as their livelihoods, be in danger, but so would the success of their flourishing local enterprises.

It was a sound view. No one could deny that. Over the years a few bold men had ridden in to challenge it, and for the most part they were now planted south-west of town upon a low knoll where the cemetery stood.

Almarjal had a reputation for being a law-and-order town. When John Billings warned his riders about going to town with chips on their shoulders he had not been motivated entirely by altruism—it was impossible to operate a cow outfit as large as JB with half a riding crew. Thad Mercer did not spend much time being sympathetic or understanding. If a rangeman got smoked up, if he even *looked* as though he might become troublesome, he went down to the cells and got locked in. He either *walked* down there disarmed and cowed, or he went down there like a sack of wet grain being carried by four other men, but he went.

But despite his unbending dedication and his hawk-like watchfulness, Thad Mercer was neither a cruel nor needlessly abusive lawman. He simply understood exactly what was required and he did it. And without any question at all, his attitude, plus the support of local folks were what kept the town and the yonder countryside from having as much trouble as other areas had.

Then Almarjal's bank was robbed.

There was not a single gunshot, four customers were at the wickets making either deposits or withdrawals, Blaine Harper was at his desk expansively fondling the great gold watch-chain which crossed his paunch from one vest-pocket to the other vest-pocket, and a smiling rangeman with whiskers—about a month's growth of them, sort of sandy-tan in colour—leaned with a bandaged hand and arm, smiling warmly, his blue eyes unblinkingly regarding Sam Trotter the chief clerk, and softly spoke as he shoved across a neatly folded little flour sack.

"Empty the drawer of paper money into the sack, mister, and do it slow, and keep smiling. *Keep smiling!*"

The bandaged hand and arm atop the counter were pushed gently past the front of the wicket. There was a gunbarrel, no more than two inches of it, showing out of the bandage.

"*Keep smiling* you son of a bitch or I'll blow your head off!"

Sam Trotter turned white to the hairline. He smoothed out the little flour sack, scarcely noticed white flour on his hands as he did so, then Sam smiled and pulled out the drawer.

There was a loaded sixgun there. In every cash-drawer in the bank as well as in the back-wall safe, there was such a weapon. Blaine Harper had boasted that given half a chance, just a little warning, his bank-people would handle any robber who thought he'd get away with it.

Sam Trotter did not even glance at the weapon. He methodically stuffed greenbacks into the flour sack—and kept smiling.

Over by the door a grizzled cowman boomed out a greeting to someone, then laughed. Everything inside the bank was normal; a little noisy and bustling, but normal, and when Sam Trotter folded the top of the floursack over and placed it atop the counter, he looked directly into the congenial face of the whiskered bank-robber. "That's all," he said in a husky voice.

The bandit's smile broadened. "Now then, friend, it's time for you to go down to the cafe for dinner. Like you always do, close the wicket, look over at old 'possum-belly yonder fiddlin' with his watch-chain, nod your head and walk out here. ... Mister, you better move natural and easy and not open your mouth. Now—walk!"

Sam obeyed to the letter. Blaine Harper nodded back in acknowledgement and spun his chair to gaze out into the busy sun-bright roadway as Sam stepped from behind the counter. The rangeman with his bandaged hand and arm was there to hold the door with a show of respect. Trotter passed through as he had been doing for almost thirty years, but this time instead of turning southward towards the cafe he hesitated until the rangeman took his arm and turned northward. They went up as far as the first intersection then the rangeman turned right and went over to the mouth of the east-side back-alley, hit Sam over the head with his bandaged arm, and stepped over the body, briskly hiking towards a sorrel saddlehorse which was drowsing in tree-shade.

He rode at a little stiff jog east beyond the last residence, then continued in that direction for another mile until he was beyond sight from town, and then he turned abruptly northward, broke over into a long lope and kept at it towards the distant foothills.

His escape was perfect and for a very good reason. Until Sam Trotter recovered from being knocked unconscious no one had any idea that a robbery had been committed. Sam groped his way to a bench around in front of the harness shop and sat with his pounding head in both hands until someone noticed him, thought he was drunk in midday, and would not go near him in candid disgust until they met Thad Mercer upon the opposite side of the road and could not refrain from making an indignant accusation.

By the time Thad got over there, learned what had really happened and had helped Sam over to Doctor Hightower's place, left him and hastened over to the bank, the outlaw was no longer anywhere near Almarjal.

Blaine Harper would not believe it. Not even after he went over and looked into Trotter's cash-drawer and found only silver and some cheques. Nor did it help that none of the other clerks had seen anything at all unusual. Sam had been working at his wicket all morning, one customer after another. No one recalled his last customer although a man who did book-keeping remembered seeing a bearded young cowboy with his hand and arm in some kind of bulky bandage outside the counter at about the time Sam Trotter was due to go out for his midday meal.

That description did not sound much like the kind of person likely to be involved in a bank-robbery.

There were no other descriptions. A lot of people had been in the bank, as usual. Mostly, they had known one another. In fact an agitated local storekeeper who was afraid he might have lost his savings in the robbery, sidled over to the jailhouse office and confronted Thad Mercer with an accusation against Sam Trotter.

Thad had scoffed. "What the hell are you talking about? According to Blaine and the book-keeper the bandit made off with three thousand dollars. Over the past twenty or more years Sam's had chances to handle three times that much money any number of times. If he'd been going to rob the bank why wouldn't he have done it when there was a lot more money around?"

But whether Sam had had better opportunities or not, three thousand dollars was more than anyone in town including Blaine Harper and the proprietor of the thriving general store made in two years. It was a fortune. The bank had quite a bit more money on hand—in the safe—but even so, the loss of three thousand dollars stunned folks nearly as much as the fact that their bank had been robbed, and also, the fact that it had been robbed without anyone being shot, without any dash out of town by gun-firing horsemen, without any excitement at all, in fact.

The rumour concerning Sam Trotter went the rounds, primarily one could suppose, because of the circumstances surrounding the robbery. Bank-robbers were supposed to ride into town, leave one man out front with the horses while the rest of the gang went inside, maybe killed a person or two, intimidated everyone else, then tried to run for it guns in one hand, bags of money in the other.

When old John Billings heard about it he said, "Gawddamnedest thing I ever heard of. Not a shot fired? Why hell, that's no bank-robbery, that's some kind of monkey business. I got to ride in and see Blaine."

He might have added that he had quite a healthy amount of money in the Stockman's Trust & Savings Bank. So had just about every other successful cow rancher in the community, along with most of the merchants and a great number of local people who were just simply frugal.

Thad Mercer was not in town when old Billings rode in. He had talked to a pair of young boys who had been rummaging trash-barrels in the back-alley and had witnessed the assault upon Sam Trotter. They had not got a close look at the man with the bandaged hand and arm but they had seen him coldcock Sam and afterwards they had been too frightened to go up there, but they had climbed through a sagging old fence and had run around where they could watch the outlaw ride away.

Thad was now out there following those fresh shod-horse marks. He was not very hopeful. There was nothing distinctive about the tracks except that they were very fresh. Otherwise, shod-horse marks were imprinted all around town by the hundreds.

Thad kept his mount in a steady slow lope in order to keep up with the freshly-turned earth, but out where the rider had gone north, the tracks were drying out, and a mile northward, they were completely obliterated where someone had driven a little gather of cattle from east to west across the range.

Sam Trotter's assailant, the only man to ever successfully rob the Stockman's Trust & Savings Bank of Almarjal, New Mexico Territory, had

BK#	PAGE	STATUS			11	12	13	14	15	16	17	18	19	20	21	22	23	24	25
		NEW							D	E		G					M		
131	25	NS	RNL		B	C	D	E	F		H		J						
132	24	NS	P/C	A	B	C	D	E	F	G					L				
132	31		RNL																
		NEW					C	D		F		H		J					
132	32	NS				B		D	E	F		H		J					
		NEW						D		F	G	H		J			M		
		NEW		A	B	C	D	E	F	G	H	I	J					
128	84	NSP	RNL			C	D		F	G	H							
132	85		RNL								H		J					
132	308					C	D	E		G	H	I	J					
131	121		RNL															

disappeared northward in the direction of the distant hills.

3

SOMETHING ...

Blaine Harper had gone through a phase of shock, a phase of stunned, befuddled disbelief, then a phase of furious indignation when he had not blamed Sam Trotter for having a hand in the actual robbery despite that rumour going the rounds, but he *had* upbraided Sam for not grabbing that loaded handgun in his cash-drawer.

Finally, he visited the jailhouse office and had a cup of bitter coffee with the constable, grey in the face and demoralised as he said, "How in the hell could that feller *do* that? It just went along as though there wasn't any way under the sun for anything to go wrong, Thad. And just one of them ... What about that gun wrapped inside the bandage; did you ever hear of anything like that before?"

Mercer could not recall right at the moment whether he'd ever encountered this ruse before, or had heard it mentioned, or had read of it being employed. He finished at the wood-stove and handed the banker one of the cups of coffee.

"And he disappeared," stated Blaine Harper, gazing up over the cup's rim. "How could that be?"

"Easy," replied Constable Mercer. "Until Sam

came round no one had any reason to think there'd been a robbery, Mister Harper, and Sam was unconscious for at least fifteen minutes."

Thad sipped coffee. He was tired. It was past suppertime, he had not eaten yet, and he'd only returned from trying to track the bank-robber a few minutes before Harper had arrived at the jailhouse.

"Luck, by gawd," muttered Harper, leaning to drink so that if coffee ran down his chin it would not stain the cloth stretched over his paunch. "Everything worked out just perfect for that bastard." He leaned back to run a sleeve across his mouth and chin. "That money belonged to folks who worked hard for it, Thad. It's things like this keep a man from believing very much in God."

Constable Mercer let that go past. He had no intention of defending God this evening. What he really wanted was for Harper to leave so Thad could lock up for the night and head for the boarding-house where he kept rooms. He was at a dead-end and experience had taught him long ago that when a man just simply could do nothing, a good night's sleep could work wonders. Also, he had not been twenty-five years old in a long time; he could no longer keep going on strength and resolve, nor did he want to keep going like that any more.

Blaine Harper cocked an eye. "You're quiet," he said. "You got something up your sleeve?"

Thad smiled and ruefully shook his head. "I don't have anything to go on at all. Just Sam's description of a feller with a beard, about six feet tall, blue-eyed, brown hair, needed a haircut. Mister Harper, that could fit half the men in the outlying cow-camps."

"And he went towards the hills, northward."

Thad shrugged that off. "He *started out* like he was going up there. Someone was moving cattle on Billings's east range and that's where I lost his tracks. But I wouldn't have been able to keep them in sight much longer anyway; they were drying out, and once that happened they'd blend with hundreds of other tracks."

"But he'd sure as the devil head for the mountains," insisted Blaine Harper. "That'd be the logical way for him to try and escape. You can't see a mounted man once he gets into the foothills, but anywhere else down here it's flat country."

Thad could agree with this logic because on the ride back he'd entertained the identical idea for the identical reasons. Now, all he said was: "In the morning I'll head up through there. It may take me a day or two, but if he left a camp up there, or if I can find some pothunters up there who might have seen him, I'll keep on the trail. Mister Harper, that's going to leave the town without a lawman."

The banker was not very worried. He was Chairman of the Almarjal Town Council, and presumably he spoke from that position when he said, "We can look after things. Thad, you'd ought to take a posse with you."

Mercer's expression remained genial—with an effort. Blaine Harper had never been anything but a townsman, and most of that time he'd spent inside a bank. How would any of that qualify him as an authority on what lawmen in pursuit of outlaws should do? It wouldn't, but on the other hand he *was* head of the Town Council.

"I'll give it some thought," replied the lawman and very pointedly pulled forth his pocket-watch, flipped open the case and steadily surveyed the position of those delicate little spidery black hands.

Blaine Harper arose, put the empty cup atop Mercer's untidy desk and brought forth a large handkerchief to wipe his hands upon as he said, "I haven't had a chance to sit down with the other fellers involved with the bank, but I think we'll be offering a reward. I'll let you know in a day or two. And Thad—you could fetch him back belly-down over his saddle and it would be just fine with me. Good night."

"Good night, Mister Harper."

Thad Mercer's mood was compatible with the banker's final suggestion but first Thad had to find the outlaw.

On his way up to the boarding-house he avoided the saloon where he might ordinarily have stopped in for a nightcap. He only made one stop, at the cafe, and because it was so late there were no other diners, for which he was grateful since he had no further desire to discuss the bank-robbery, the only topic of conversation in town tonight, and for the next few days as news of the robbery travelled farther out, like a stone dropped into a pond, the only topic at the distant cow-camps as well.

He nodded to several smokers in the gloom of the boarding-house front porch, did not stop because he realised they were waiting to see if he would, so they could start firing questions, but went straight on up to his room.

Something troubled him, but being tired acted as

an opiate. He knew there was something floating loose inside his head and could not pin it down. It was there, gently nagging, when he retired and when he opened his eyes in the pre-dawn greyness it was still there, still nagging.

At the cafe a bulky, dark man named Winters, who owned and operated the general store, got red in the face just at the sight of Town Marshal Thad Mercer. There were other diners along the counter and they too looked upon the lawman with fresh interest. Most of them Mercer had known ever since he'd hired on in Almarjal as local lawman, had stood up at the bar with them, had exchanged ribald jokes down in front of the liverybarn with them, had attended Fourth of July celebrations and New Year's dances with them. But this morning they gazed at him as though they were half ready to believe he was not doing the job he was being paid for.

At least he had that feeling as he strolled to the lower end of the counter and sat, then caught the cafeman's eye and nodded. He had been eating the same breakfast in here for a lot of years. It was an on-going joke between Mercer and the cafeman. This morning he got back a nod and that was all.

Walter Winters leaned and said, "You turn up anything yesterday, Thad?"

Every head came up and turned. Thad answered warily. "Not much, Walter. Nightfall came on me and I had to head back."

"But you'll be heading out again this morning, eh? But you know, Thad, if that son of a bitch didn't camp last night, he could be fifty miles away by now. Maybe, if you'd stayed on his trail. ..."

Mercer did not have to answer, a shaggy-headed, faded and worn-looking elder rangeman peered sceptically at Walt Winters, fork upright in one fist, knife upright in the other. "In the dark without no moon, mister, and not havin' no idea where the feller was headin' once he got up into them hills?"

The cowboy kept regarding Walt Winters after he had made his sarcastic observation. Then he wagged his head in obvious disgust and went back to his breakfast.

The storekeeper, who was a very dark, burly man, shifted his attention. He had been mildly ridiculed before all the other diners. On the other hand, that scruffy-looking rangerider wore an ivory-stocked sixgun and did not have the appearance of an individual who would stand for much chousing.

The cook came with Mercer's breakfast, set it down and wordlessly turned away. Other diners came in, a few went out, and when Walt Winters left he leaned beside the lawman and quietly said, "Take him with you; he acts like a man who might be handy to have along on a manhunt."

Winters left and a few moments later so did Thad Mercer. He did not expect to see that greying, run-down-looking rangerider again. Nor did he.

The morning had some of autumn's magnificent colours spread among the trees around town, and far out where the foothills rose softly, there was a soft-blurred haze with a bluish tint. Blue-grey, as though there had been a forest fire miles distant, and that haze were the residue of the smoke's wind-driven drift.

Doctor Hightower was sitting comfortably upon

the bench out front when Thad came over to unlock his jailhouse door.

It seemed a little unusual, Doc sitting there. Normally, he was busy in the mornings. For some obscure reason when children came down with things like summer complaint or the croup or measles and mumps, it was in the morning.

Doc was smoking a thin dark cigar and although he had not been a young man in many years, each morning after he had scrubbed and shaved, his face looked almost cherubic. Not until later in the day did he begin to look older and begin to act older.

Thad stopped, key in hand. They exchanged a look, then Abe Hightower removed his cigar to say, "It's an old complaint with you by now, Thad. I lost my savings in that robbery yesterday. I'm in no way accusing you—I just want to know my chances of getting them back."

Mercer sighed, bent to unlock the door, pushed it inward and gestured. "Come inside, Doc."

The jailhouse was clammy-cold, as it was almost every morning excepting of course during the tag-end of the hot summers. Thad got a fire going in the wood-stove, set his graniteware coffeepot atop the only stove-burner, then pitched down his hat at the desk and faced Doc Hightower.

"I'll tell you something I can't tell other folks. Not very many of them anyway. Catching a bank-robber once he gets clear of you, just don't happen. Not once out of a hundred cases. Doc; I'll do every lousy thing I can. This morning I'm going into the hills and try to pick up more sign."

Hightower's shrewd, wise eyes did not leave the

marshal's face. "But you expect to ride your tail off for nothing."

"If there is any way under the sun to get onto that man's trail and run him to earth," said Mercer, leaning to sit down, "I expect to do it. I told Mister Harper I might be out of town for a spell."

Hightower was a humane individual so now he said, "Mind what you ride into, and don't get killed over a measly three thousand dollars." His shrewd gaze lingered. "Whatever Walt Winters will say— pay it no mind. Him and a lot of other folks." The medical practitioner arose. "I didn't have that much in savings anyway—four hundred dollars." He winked and turned to depart, looked from a fly-specked front window and raised tufted eyebrows. "Old John Billings out there with his rangeboss and half his riding crew. That's an unusual sight. Old skinflint don't ordinarily bring anyone to town with him for fear he won't get a full day's work out of 'em. Well; remember what I told you," he muttered, and walked out just as big old cold-eyed John Billings shouldered past and walked in looking bleak.

Mercer had his hat in his hand. He did not want to be delayed any more than he already had been, so the moment the big old cowman entered he said, "I'm on my way out, Mister Billings. I'd like to make it to the foothills before noon, if possible."

The tough-faced rancher stood listening to all that while tugging off riding gloves. He did not raise his head until his rangeboss and three of his riders had also crowded inside. They were all fairly large men, and this morning they were bundled against a little unseasonal dawn chill so that made them seem even larger.

"You can wait," stated Billings in a rough tone as he shoved folded gloves under his shellbelt. "We was raided last night, Marshal."

Thad stared at the old man, then looked at his riders, read the identical expression on each face and turned back to say, "Rustlers?"

Instead of a reply the cowman, with his head still slightly lowered, said, "I only saw the one feller but there was more. I heard them riding off westerly. Sounded like maybe three men."

Thad stared. "They robbed the ranch?"

"Took twenty-five hundred dollars from my strongbox, knocked me over the head, but I came round and played 'possum while he was ransackin' the desk and the cabinets. When he left out the back window I tried to get up to get m'gun and couldn't make it—got dizzy in the head and kept falling back down."

The rangeboss said, "We tried to track him but had to give up until morning." He shrugged. "It wasn't no good, by then. Except that we figured there really was three of them. The horses was kept out a-ways. One feller stayed with them. Another feller hid round the corner of the well-house. We picked up his sign easy, where he run back to the horses. We figure he was coverin' the bunkhouse in case we busted out of there. The third feller was inside the main-house." The rangeboss made a hand-gesture. "No beginners did that, Marshal, not by a damned sight."

Billings went to a bench and sat down. He did not

look as though he had recently been struck down, but evidently he was still not back to normal. "I want those men," he gruffly said. "Marshal, I'll give two hundred dollars a head for them."

Thad reached in a shirt-pocket for his makings and started rolling a smoke. That nagging little vagueness was back to pester him as he made the cigarette and lit it, then faced John Billings to ask a question.

"What time last night?"

"This morning," growled the cowman. "Three o'clock. That's what m'watch said when I finally could stand up and light a lamp. Three o'clock in the morning, Thad."

Mercer had another question; one which earned a blank look from Billings and his riders. "Why did you move some cattle from east of the stageroad yesterday to the west side?"

The rangeboss said, "Move cattle ...? For Chris' sake what's that got to do with Mister Billings gettin' near killed last night?"

Thad waited, eyed the rangeboss stiffly, then turned towards the cowman again. "Why did you move those cattle, Mister Billings?"

The cowman raised a puzzled face to his rangeboss. "What the hell cattle is he talkin' about?"

The rangeboss did not know. "We never moved no cattle yesterday, nor the day before that, nor for that matter for this past month, from over east of town to the home range. We don't do that until later in the autumn."

Thad trickled smoke. "No one from your crew pushed a little band of cattle from the east range over to the west range yesterday? You are damned sure of that, are you?"

"Positive," exclaimed the rangeboss, and when Thad stood in thoughtful silence, the rangeboss then reverted to his earlier concern. "And what's it got to do with Mister Billings gettin' robbed—anyway?"

Maybe there was no connection. Thad leaned to punch out his cigarette. The little nagging doubt in the back of his mind was at rest, now. Last night there had been *something*, but not until ten minutes ago had it crystallised and come down where he could examine it.

It had been a question: those cattle which had been driven over the tracks of the escaping bank-robber— had they been deliberately used to mask the fleeing man's tracks?

Evidently they had. Billings and his rangeboss had just confirmed that they had. Thad raised his face. There was something going on; clearly, despite what Blaine Harper and everyone else believed, that bank-robbery had not been the work of just one man with a gun hidden inside a bandage on his hand and arm.

And this morning, another solitary outlaw had robbed Old Man Billings. Only it had turned out not to be just one man.

Thad said, "I'll do what I can," and put on his hat, then stood waiting. Billings and his riders took their cue from the look on the lawman's face. They filed out ahead of him and when he turned away, in the direction of the livery barn, they silently watched him go.

4

REACTIONS

He did not ride into the foothills, he returned to that area where those cattle had been driven from east to west, traced their route without difficulty and found that they had been abandoned just short of the stageroad and in fact were still over there, strung out a little now, but still over there.

Then he turned back to pick up the sign of the horses which had been behind the drive. It took longer to make a pretty good guess but he came up with what were two distinct sets of tracks.

Three men, one to rob the bank, the other two in position to make certain the robber escaped. There was a good chance they had sat their saddles keeping an eye on the solitary horseman who rushed forth— too late—from town. If that were true, if they had been watching, it was probably a good thing Thad had not got any closer to the bank-robber.

So much for that. He dismounted in the shade of a tree to roll and light a smoke, and to look in all directions out across seemingly endless miles of emptiness. Between Almarjal and the northward foothills there was nothing but open range. There were ranches out there, and a number of seasonal cow-camps too, but they were not visible from where Thad Mercer was idly smoking as he arrived at some unsupportable conclusions.

Their method of operating was the same in both robberies, except that at the Billings ranch they had used violence. Old John had been knocked over the head. Well; knowing Billings made it seem plausible that he had either cursed the outlaw or had in some other way antagonised the man.

Maybe not. Maybe the outlaw had simply struck Billings down to avoid the possibility of a bullet in the back.

But they had operated the same way. One man had gone forward to commit the robbery, the other two had lain back waiting and watching. What would have happened if the riders had busted out of the bunkhouse?

Murder pure and simple. Otherwise, why would that man have been hiding in the darkness at the corner, the way the rangeboss reported.

So far no one had been seriously injured. Thad dropped the smoke and turned to mount up. So far. If those men struck a few more times, and sure as hell they would, and someone stood up to them. ...

He turned to ride on around the countryside to the west, and south-west, of the stageroad. Why would they strike again? Because they had just made the easiest wages and the most money they had likely ever seen in their damned lives—all over one twenty-four-hour period.

By early afternoon he was in the yard of the Billings ranch, and the old cowman came forth from a belated midday meal still with the napkin tucked under his chin to glower and say, "You found anything yet?"

Thad ignored that to ask a question of his own. "That man who raided you, Mister Billings: whiskery, tallish, blue-eyed man with—"

"He was dark-eyed, dark-haired, had dark whiskers and was no more'n average build, but husky. Maybe in his mid-twenties." The old man pulled loose his napkin and leaned on the porch railing looking at the lawman on his horse. "You got some notion about one of them, have you?"

"Maybe."

"Well, that feller you're thinking about could have been the one out with their horses, or the one over watchin' the bunkhouse."

Thad nodded. He hadn't required that suggestion but he nodded and thanked the cowman, raised his hand in a little salute and rode out of the yard westerly.

Reading sign on the JB outfit was like looking at grains of sand along a seashore, but he sashayed back and forth for an hour anyway before striking out straight west in the hope of picking up the tracks of three men riding together, fast.

What he turned up was dozens of criss-crossing shod-horse marks of JB riders, very often riding in pairs or in threes.

He turned back with the sun reddening as it sank lower towards the far bend of the earth, and deliberately skirted around and below the Billings yard again.

He reached town after nightfall, which in a sense was favourable, had another late supper at the cafe then went over to his office to try and ferret his way through the stack of wanted posters over there, in the hope of locating some outlaws who operated as a trio and who might be concerned solely with robberies.

What he turned up was a dusty stack of nothing, so he had a smoke as he strolled northward to the boarding-house.

This night he did not sleep as well as he had the previous night. This night he knew *something*, or thought he knew something anyway—*suspected* something at any rate—and the tantalising aspect of it was that what he knew or what he suspected was not information which he could pin upon any particular individual, or any particular trio of individuals.

What he had to do, clearly, was locate three men who were capable of committing clever robberies, and that was about like trying to rope calves in the dark—a man expended a heap of effort and pulled back an empty loop every time.

In the morning he encountered Blaine Harper over in front of the general store. Blaine had been in conversation with Walter Winters, but Walt went inside and as the banker turned and caught sight of Thad Mercer, he stood there waiting.

Thad felt like sighing. Instead he smiled and greeted the banker amiably, then braced for what he knew was coming.

"You got back already from the foothills, Thad? I figured it might take you a couple more days to run him down."

Thad continued to smile. "You heard what happened to Mister Billings?"

"Yes, and I'd like to know what this territory is

coming to, folks being choused right out of their beds and robbed in their homes."

"I didn't get into the foothills yesterday, Mister Harper, I investigated the Billings robbery instead."

Blaine Harper's heavy features gradually smoothed out into an expression of veiled antagonism. He cleared his throat first, then spoke again in a quieter, almost soft, tone of voice.

"Thad, Mister Billings's a pillar in our area, no doubt about that, and I certainly meant what I just said about the outrage of folks being choused out of their beds to be robbed and all—but—the bank's loss was bigger, you know, and there was a lot more folks got hurt when the bank lost that three thousand dollars. What I'm tryin' to get across to you, Mercer, is that the Town Council and the folks around here who voted you in at the last election—all those folks want to see that son of a bitchin' bank-robber brought in."

Thad could feel colour creeping up from his neck. Blaine Harper was not an individual he had ever really cared much for. He respected Harper because of his position with the bank, and because of his other civic affiliations, but as a *man* he did not much care for Harper at all.

That was what made it difficult now to take that rebuke without flaring back. But Thad was not twenty-five either, so a lot of the sharp edge to his disposition had been dulled with the passage of time. This made it easier for him to maintain dogged silence until the fiery feeling had passed, and then to say, "I do my job to the best of my ability, Mister

Harper. If there's a way to bring in your man, I'll do it."

Then he turned, stepped down into roadway dust and went walking a trifle stiffly over towards the jailhouse. He did not quite make it. Doc Hightower was emerging from the gun shop north of the jailhouse, saw Thad, and turned to walk down and stop him out front as he said, "I was watching you and Blaine through the window next door just now." Doc lifted a long upper lip in a simulated smile. "I got the impression he nettled you a mite. Son, as I told you yesterday—don't let him do that to you. He is a bully, that's all he is. If he can bluster and stamp around and intimidate folks he does it. I've known him a lot longer than you have so I can safely say— don't let him hoorawh you."

Thad smiled. "I'll take your advice, Doc, but all the same, someday I'd like to punch him right in the nose."

"Paunch, son, in the paunch; won't injure your knuckles." Doc winked and went strolling southward in the direction of the buggy works. He had his rig down there; three days back in a rush to get back to town ahead of nightfall after delivering a ranch-baby, Doc had straddled a boulder and had bent both axles. And there went all he'd made by delivering the baby.

Well hell, there were no guarantees in this lousy vale of tears. Invariably just when a man thought he was winning, something like two bent axles turned up. For Thad Mercer it was not bent axles it was Blaine Harper, but that too faded as the day wore along. It did not entirely leave the back of Thad's mind for the full day simply because he was that kind of an individual. The kind that kept a lot inside himself. But he almost forgot about it when Sam Trotter came over to the jailhouse office on his dinner break at high noon, and wanted to know if Thad had made any progress. Sam's interest, he was quick to explain, was not entirely the same as Mister Harper's interest. Of course Sam wanted the bank to get its money back; after all Sam had been connected with the bank since John Billings and a few other rangemen—all dead now except old Billings—had founded the institution, and he felt a good bit of loyalty to an outfit which had paid him month in and month out, good weather and bad, for all those years. But what he revealed to Thad was that what he truly wanted was revenge for being frightened half to death like that, and also for then being knocked senseless.

And there was a small sense of guilt too, as when he said, "I could have picked up the gun. It was only six inches from my fingers when I was emptying my money-drawer for that bandit. Thad, it was loaded and all, and I just—well—"

"Forget it," admonished the lawman. "Sam, if you'd so much as moved your hand those six inches he'd have killed you sure as hell. Don't never—you listen to me, Sam, just in case this ever happens again—don't you never reach for a gun when you are already under someone else's gun. You hear? No man that I ever heard of beat drawing against a royal flush—cards or Colts. What the hell good would you have been dead—he'd have got that flour sack full of greenbacks anyway."

"My hand was sweating like blue-blazes," stated

the bank clerk, looking at the hands in his lap. "But the flour from the sack sopped up some of it." He raised troubled eyes. "Yeah, I know you're right, Thad, but—well—in all my life I've just never had to prove nothing. You see?"

Marshal Mercer considered the clerk, and smiled at him. "You're a man," he said, beginning to smile a little. "What do you have to prove that you and I don't already know? You'd have got yourself shot down, Sam, for what? Hell's bells, you're brave enough without having to commit suicide to prove it. And after you are dead you wouldn't be able to hear anyone say Sam Trotter was a brave man, anyway."

Thad went to the stove. "Care for some coffee?" he asked, and got a head-wag from the bank clerk. "Don't drink it. Never learned to like it, Marshal, and that's something else. I've never worked on the range, in a cow-camp, never rode a bucking horse ..." Trotter arose. "Well; I guess I been saying a lot of stuff I hadn't ought to have." He levered up a feeble smile. "Excuse me, Thad."

Mercer crossed to the door and held it open, and as the clerk stepped through he slapped him on the shoulder. Sam turned in the shade of the front-wall overhang and said, "I didn't mean to take up so much of your time. I'm plumb obliged for you listening, Thad."

Mercer nodded. "Any time you want to talk, come on back ... Hey Sam! Just a minute!" Thad stepped out upon the duckboards facing the clerk. "What did you say about your hand sweating?"

Trotter blinked. "Sweating ...? Oh; flour-dust from that little sack the robber gave me to shove the money into, sopped up most of the sweat. Afterwards I had to dry my hands on a handkerchief."

Thad stood gazing steadily at Trotter for a moment longer, then gave him another slap on the shoulder and dismissed him. For a short while the lawman simply stood gazing up the roadway, then he stepped to the wall-bench out front, sat down and thumbed back his hat as he thoughtfully went to work rolling a smoke.

The day was wearing along pleasantly, now and then a rig, either a buggy or a ranch-wagon, scuffed dust out in the roadway, and an occasional horseman moving either up from the south or down from the north, came along.

Most of the tie-racks out front of the business establishments had a saddle animal or a rig tethered in the pleasant warmth, and there were people moving to and fro on both sides of the roadway. It was a typical autumn day in Almarjal except for the way Marshal Mercer was smoking and staring narrowly across the road and up northward a few doors in the direction of the flourishing general store.

5

THE INTERIM

Walter Winters was one of those successful merchants who could be said not to have a personality. Whatever Walt may have been in his younger, less inhibited days, had somewhere along the road to greying maturity shrivelled up and departed.

Walt's entire life was inside the four walls of his big store building. At social gatherings such as the Independence Day celebrations, or the Christmas festivities over at the school, Walt could be counted upon to show up, because he was conscious of his civic responsibility, and he could also be counted upon to smile and applaud when he was supposed to, but in a conversation about the price of cattle, the condition of the range, the weather or national matters, Walt showed up tongue-tied and unable to have an idea. He could discuss prices of dry goods though, or tinned food, or grain and tools all day long.

He was a widower, and some folks said that after the death of his wife Walter had thrown himself into his work at the store with such ferocity that he had indeed managed to forget, but at the expense of having become a fanatic as a storekeeper.

Maybe that was true. Thad Mercer did not know and did not particularly care. His personal reaction to Walter was about as it was to some other people around town—he knew them, got along well enough with them, had almost nothing at all in common with them, and when he had occasion to speak to them he did so strictly in the manner of someone doing his duty.

That was how he sat now in Walter's cubby-hole of a dingy little office listening as Walter said, "What you're askin', Marshal, is a tall order. Not hardly a day goes by folks don't show up here to buy sacks of flour. Why, just this morning some riders came in with the ranch-wagon from the Corby outfit and taken on three hundred pounds. And yesterday we sold—"

"Walter," exclaimed the lawman quietly. "I'm not interested in who bought three hundred pounds of flour. I'm not even interested in who bought one hundred pounds. As for all those folks buying flour—I'm glad for you—but the information I'm asking for is who do you recall buying one of those little two or three pound sacks of flour rangemen buy to carry with them as they travel along. The *little* sacks, Walter, not the big ones. Who over the past few days—maybe the past week—can you recall buying one of those little sacks of flour?"

Winters threw up his hands. This sort of thing aggravated him, especially during store-hours, so he said, "Marshal, they come in and they go on out again. In the spring and autumn rangeriders are forever passing through, you know that. How could anyone be expected to remember who he sold a little sack of flour to? And there's only a few cents profit—you understand? A man in business can't be expected to clutter up his mind with things like that. It's the *big* purchases that make me a living, not those little ones."

Thad sighed, his patience slipping a notch. "Walter—just remember one man buying one of those little sacks."

"Why is it all this important, Marshal?"

"Because it was one of those little sacks which was used by that outlaw when he raided the bank, that's why."

Winters threw his arms wide. "My gawd, Marshal, every blessed town in the territory sells those little sacks of flour. That son of a bitch could have got his flour-sack anywhere."

"But I don't think he did, Walter."

"Why not? Just tell me that. Why not?"

"Because it was a fresh sack; had been holding flour only maybe the very day before the robbery. When Sam Trotter was handed the sack and handled it, flour-dust got all over his hands. My guess is that someone only bought that sack a few days earlier, Walter, and when he came to town with it—"

"Yes, I see," broke in the storekeeper. "Yes indeed." He turned to briefly stare at Thad. "That's using your head. All right—give me a little time to try and remember. I'll come over to your office later on. All right?"

It was all right because clearly it was going to have to be all right. What Thad had hoped for was no argument, just a quick recollection and a description. He could still hope for those two things but as he stood out front of the general store he had to be satisfied that there was not going to be any swift description.

It was tantalising to have to wait, but there was one interlude which helped pass the time and which also came close to making him forget about Walter Winters.

John Billings arrived in town, alone this time, and after spending an hour up at the bank with Blaine Harper, the old cowman came along to take a chair in Mercer's office and to forthrightly say, "We got to have some activity about these here holdups, Marshal. You setting around in town all the time just don't look good to folks."

Thad smiled. "I can't braid you a bandit, Mister Billings."

"I don't need any smart-ass answers from you, Marshal," exclaimed the older man, and for the first time Thad Mercer flared up.

He stood up at the desk. "I'm going to tell you something, Mister Billings—just once. I'm doing the best I can do. If it's not good enough and you think you or Mister Harper can do better—get the Council to fire me, then take it over, the whole damned mess, and do it your own way. Otherwise, don't you walk in here again actin' like it's my fault; you were enough of a damned fool to keep twenty-five hundred dollars in your strongbox at the ranch!"

Billings blinked slowly, stared for a silent long moment then cleared his throat. In icy tones he said, "In case you don't know it, Marshal, a cow outfit as big as mine runs on greenbacks. I'm paying riders every week and I'm hirin' horses broke, hay hauled in, shoeing done—the whole damned thing runs on greenbacks, therefore I got to keep enough of them on hand ... Now if you want to make trouble for—"

"Wait a minute," said Thad, leaning against the desk. "All these years you've kept that much money in your strongbox at the ranch?"

"Yes. I just told you what I had to—"

"And has anyone ever raided you before?"

"Never, Marshal. Nor do I figure it would be the smartest things fellers could try to do. I keep loaded guns all over the main-house and I don't hire no riders who wouldn't fight for the brand that's paying them."

"But they've known, Mister Billings. You've had men over the years who have known you kept a lot of money in the house?"

"Of course they've known. I never yet had to send my crew to a damned bank to get paid. I'm no shoe-string cowman ... And so you're figuring that someone who knew, came back the other night ... Marshal; I had plenty of time to look at that feller. I never saw him before in my life. Never. For a fact he never rode for JB. I may be gettin' along but sure as hell I never forget a face. That thieving son of a bitch was a total stranger to me."

Thad sat back down. "He wouldn't have had to work for you. Riders who have rode for JB could have told the story of you paying off in cash all season long in a hundred different towns and camps. Someone who heard that yarn—some *three* fellers who heard it, Mister Billings, could be out there right now—after having hit you, and having also hit the bank."

"Only one man raided the bank, damn it all!"

"Damn it all," shot back Thad. "One man *went inside the bank*, Mister Billings, but there were three of them all told!"

The old man leaned back along the wall steadily regarding Thad Mercer. After a time he said, "Are you sure of that?"

"I'm confident of it," replied Thad.

"How—you only rode out of town yesterday according to Blaine and others around town," stated Billings. "The rest of the time you been right here."

"Mister Billings, when you want to know about me—don't ask other folks, come and ask me."

Thad went around his desk to the door, opened it and left it open, then went wordlessly back behind the desk to sit and bleakly regard his rich and powerful visitor. For some time not a word was spoken, then Billings finally arose and went as far as the door before turning to say, "The same band each time?"

Thad nodded and still did not open his mouth.

Billings wagged his head in the manner of an annoyed old bull in fly time. "How'd you come onto that, staying around town?" He turned and went clumping southward in the direction of the livery-barn, and because he had come off second best at the constable's office, something he was not accustomed to at all, and something which stoked the fires of his natural short-fused irritability, when he found that his horse had been grained and hayed but not cuffed, he went fiercely in search of the liveryman to say, "By gawd when folks come in here and pay you good money for services, they expect to get them. Look at that horse! No one's laid a currycomb nor a brush on his back at all. Confound you anyway, I got a good notion to fetch in some of my riders to teach you lessons in honesty! Now clean up that horse, damn your lousy lights, and rig him out and fetch him up to me at the saloon—you hear?"

He stamped back out, crossed the road and went stumping northward looking mean and black-visaged.

Blaine Harper was standing in conversation out front of the bank. He did not see Mister Billings but the townsman he was talking to saw the old cowman marching towards them over the banker's shoulder. He said, "Well; I'm due over at the stage office, so I'll see you later," and turned to cross the road. He had reached the far side before old Billings, head lowered like a bravo bull, came up and said, "Damn you anyway, Blaine, for telling me all that crap about Mercer. He's on the job. Regardless of whether you saw him ride out or not he's on the job, which is more'n I can say for you—standing out front here chewin' the fat with any idiot who comes along when you're supposed to be inside minding things!"

Billings went on past and turned in at the saloon. Blaine Harper was immobile. During all the long years of their association he had never before had Billings speak to him like that. Never. It was as though someone had flung a whole bucketful of cold water unexpectedly into his face. He stood gasping.

Thad was emerging from his office and caught a glimpse of old Billings entering the saloon, and on this side of the old man he could see Blaine turning very slowly to also watch as Billings entered the saloon. From that distance Thad could not make out the expression upon the banker's face, but he could tell enough from the stiffly erect way in which Harper was standing. Someone had said something, and Blaine Harper could not quite get over it.

Thad did not feel any pity at all as he turned to hike across and hunt up Walt Winters again.

Walt was just leaving the store. His clerk was still as busy in there as a kitten in a box of shavings. He threw a very reproachful look in Walt's direction which neither Winters nor Thad Mercer saw.

Winters, seeing the lawman on his way over, waited in the shade of the store-front and when Thad got over there Winters said, "There was one thing. I'd forgot about it until a short while back." Winters screwed up his features. "Do you recollect a family used to live around here named Beaudry?" At Mercer's blank look the storekeeper looked even more aggravated. "I figured you wouldn't. Not many folks would. Old Man Beaudry worked as hostler around town. His missus took in washing and did mending—such like. They had a girl; she married some travelling feller and went out to California—last I heard."

Thad slowly shook his head. "Were they around here while I was?"

"Sure; in fact the old man died the year you hired on and the old woman hung on a little longer, couple more years as I recollect, then the girl left and the lad—it's the lad I'm talking about—he went off cowboying one summer. The old woman died that autumn. We buried her and that was the end of it." Walt Winters paused, then said, "Until last week. The boy walked into the store. I don't know why I should have recognised him, it'd been quite a few years and he'd grown up and changed some, but the minute he came towards me grinning I put a name to him. George Beaudry, by golly."

"And. ...?"

Winters looked briefly irritated. "And—you badgered me to remember who'd been in to buy one of those little sacks of flour. George Beaudry. He bought a two-pound sack of flour, some tinned peaches and some dried prunes. Stuff rangemen buy when they got limited space and are on the move."

"He was passing through?"

"No. Well; maybe so but he didn't say he was. We talked a little while about old times. I told him which grave belonged to his maw and he said he'd already been out there and found it ... That's about all. He didn't mention his paw nor his sister. Just mentioned having been a rangeman for the past years, like most other young bucks. Then some other customers came in and when I went back, he'd gone."

Thad said, "Any other folks buy those little bags of flour that you can also recall?"

"Asa Hedron down at the harness works. He lives in the back of his shop and since his missus passed away five, six years back—you'll remember that funeral, just about everyone for miles around attended—Asa bought some of those little sacks. Two of them. He does his own cooking." Winters pursed his lips. "I asked my clerk if he remembered any others. He didn't. So I went and counted the sacks and checked that number against our manifests. There was another two I can't account for, but that could simply mean the clerk sold 'em and forgot about it."

Thad smiled. "I'm right obliged, and if the clerk

gets his memory jogged about those other two sacks. ... ?"

"Sure. I'll keep after him and let you know." Winters turned, looked in the store-window, saw customers ganging up on his clerk, and said, "Later, Marshal. We'll talk later." He turned abruptly and hustled inside.

Thad built and lit a smoke, turned and thoughtfully considered the harness shop upon the opposite side of the road, southward, decided that even if the old saddle and harness maker needed money, even if he'd tried a few robberies, his description was all wrong this time.

But he had known Asa Hedron since arriving in Almarjal. If ever there was a firm believer in law and order, it was the harness-maker.

Thad returned to his office, pitched the smoked-down cigarette into the stove, clanged the iron door and put his hat aside as he thought back to the name Beaudry among all those names he had seen while scouting through his pile of wanted dodgers.

It had not been there, he was sure of it, nonetheless he went over and with a grunt of resignation started pawing through the posters again.

He was not at all hopeful. He was not, in fact, even remotely suspicious of George Beaudry.

6

BITS AND PIECES

The liveryman did not remember any hostler named Beaudry but Max Jeeter the yardboss for the stage company remembered Beaudry.

"He was a hard worker, and dependable," Jeeter recollected for Thad Mercer. "Drank a little—not a hell of a lot. He had a sickly woman and two spindly kids—boy and girl as I recollect. The kids taken after their paw—dark, they was, with black hair and dark eyes and all. Beaudry was one of those folk that just never managed to pull themselves up from where they started out. I don't know why. Never could figure it out, and with him—dependable and hard-workin' and all, it just didn't make no sense. Likable cuss. Yeah; he worked here for maybe a year then he taken something and got down and died. Hell yes, I remember him, Marshal. Him and me used to buy a bucket of suds between us every Saturday—payday you see—and sip on it all afternoon."

On the stroll back to his office Thad thought of those two flour sacks Walt Winters had not been able to account for, feeling inclined to put more faith in them and the people who had bought them than he was in a suspicion concerning some itinerant rangerider named George Beaudry who had most probably been simply passing through.

Then he had an impromptu thought, veered over and entered the general store just in time to catch Walt on his way out back wearing an apron and carrying a clipboard with some stained, rumpled manifests clipped in place. There was a freight wagon at the dock back there. Walt swept Thad up and brought him right along as he tried to answer Thad's question by saying, "Dark, sort of about middle height, husky built feller, got black whiskers." They reached the dock where a freighter and his swamper were idly smoking in dock-shade. The freighter was a bull-necked, grizzled man whose dark gaze showed a nettlesome disposition. He turned to watch Walt and Thad, then pushed upright, pitched away his smoke and growled at his swamper. They both walked in over the tailgate, seized heavy boxes and walked out again to begin the process of unloading.

Walt peered at labels, checked articles off on the clipboard and when Thad said, "How old would he be by now?" Winters scowled a little, annoyedly, as he answered.

"Twenty-two maybe. Possibly a year or two older. Marshal; I got to concentrate or I'll have to do this all over again. Can we talk about George Beaudry later?"

Thad departed up through the store, bought a fresh sack of tobacco and straw papers from the clerk, and went out front to stand a moment, until he saw John Billings emerge from the saloon and walk over where a hostler from the liverybarn was holding the cowman's saddle animal.

Thad started up there, trailing smoke, as Billings passed over some silver to the hostler. The liveryman immediately turned and briskly walked away. He did not seem to care to be in Billings's company one moment more than he had to be.

As Thad came up and the old man turned to slip a finger under the cincha, he saw Mercer and pulled out the finger, completed the turn and said, "You sure about that—three of 'em involved in the bank robbery?"

Thad ignored that to say, "When that outlaw was robbing you, Mister Billings, and you were looking at him—are you plumb certain you had never seen him before?"

"Well, confound it, I told you I never saw him before, didn't I?"

"Stocky man, average height, dark eyes and hair and beard—maybe in his middle twenties?"

Billings glowered. "You're repeatin' what I told you, Marshal."

Thad smiled. "Do you recollect a man named Beaudry around town here, some years back? Worked as a hostler, first at the liverybarn then up at the stage company's corralyard?"

"I recollect him," stated Billings. "I recollect when he died too. What of it?"

"His son, Mister Billings. ..."

The older man stood silently glowering for another moment before slowly straightening up. "I'll be damned," he said in a suddenly fresher tone of voice. "By gawd I think so. Older, and those whiskers made a lot of difference, but by gawd you're right. Sure as I'm standin' here that's who he was ... You know, after we talked out at the ranch and you asked if I'd seen him before, and I told you that I hadn't—you know, Thad, that sort of bothered me a little. I couldn't figure out exactly why it bothered me, right then, but I can figure it out now. Sure as hell that's who he was: Beaudry. Looked like his paw. He also had black whiskers. Shaved 'em off the last six months or so, but ... And this one looked exactly like the old man!"

Thad maintained his smile. "I'd appreciate it, Mister Billings," he said, "if you wouldn't tell anyone else this. Not anyone at all. Not your rangeboss nor anyone here in town. Not a blessed soul."

John Billings was still standing erect, and the irritable, testy look on his rugged features was gone. He stepped ahead, hooked his arms over the tie-rack beside his drowsing horse, gazed frankly at Thad Mercer and waggled his head. "I take back what I said about you, Marshal ... Thad. I sure take it back. All right; I'll not tell a blessed soul a thing. ... But he wasn't alone, was he?"

"No sir," stated Mercer. "Tell me something else. Was Blaine Harper around Almarjal when the Beaudrys lived here?"

"Yes," exclaimed the older man. "In fact Blaine was here the year before old Beaudry died, and when his missus passed on Blaine went to the funeral like everyone else. Not because he knew the old lady that well—bankers got to do things like that. It helps business ... Thad; why did you ask that?"

"Because," replied the lawman, still thinly smiling, "I'm trying to work up something."

"What—something?"

"To start with, Mister Billings—Beaudry would not rob the bank if he thought someone in there like maybe Sam Trotter or Blaine Harper would know him, would he?"

Billings pondered and solemnly agreed. "For a fact he wouldn't—if he didn't want folks to know who the robber was ... But he raided me."

"Evidently he did not believe you would know him. And you darned near didn't, Mister Billings."

Billings said nothing until Thad's smile faded as he made another observation for the benefit of the old cowman. "Three of them, Mister Billings: one raided the bank and got off with it. Another one—Beaudry—raided you, and damned near got away with it. Got off with your money, sure, but what was more important darned near got off as a stranger."

"And that leaves the third one. Is that what you're hinting, Thad?"

Mercer was indeed thinking like that. "The third one so far hasn't done much but stand watch or mind the horses. If they are working the way I figure—each one is to make a raid somewhere—there is still the man no one has seen yet."

Billings, in full grasp, now turned instantly to the topic in Thad's mind. "Where? Here in town or maybe at some cow outfit?"

If Thad could have answered that he would not have been standing talking. "Damned if I know," he frankly replied. "If you come up with anything I'll be around town somewhere." He gave Billings a moment to comment and when the cowman simply continued to lean beside his horse, Thad turned and walked away.

Thad Mercer was not ordinarily that frank about his suspicions, but there had been two reasons for him to be so this time. One reason was that he was entirely satisfied John Billings would not open his mouth to anyone; he had known the cowman long enough to appreciate just how tight-lipped the older man was.

His second reason was more elastic. He had not, himself, been even partially convinced that Beaudry was one of the outlaws until after his brief talk with Walt Winters. What he had done with John Billings was talk it out, use the shrewd old cowman as his sounding-board.

It had worked very well. So well, in fact, that now Billings *did* remember encountering the man who had robbed and assaulted him. Nor was it to be expected that Billings or most other people would have been able to recall George Beaudry as handily as Walt Winters had done it.

But Billings had made that identification, finally, and that had been another of Thad's strategies. Now, on his way southward in the pleasant autumn sunshine, he fitted several bits and pieces together so that by the time he reached his office, he was ready to assume some kind of initiative.

He made a fresh pot of coffee, sampled one cup out of it, and left the jailhouse to go south-westerly out to the local cemetery.

It was not such a vastly populated place, for although there was no denying that people had been dying like flies ever since Almarjal's citizenry had voted to establish their cemetery district, a lot of corpses were shipped elsewhere at the request of heirs, and another considerable number of those who had died had been natives, either Indians or Mexicans, or cross-breeds, and for the most part they were buried elsewhere, either over in Mex-town which had a huge old untended graveyard out behind the adobe church, or discreetly and in some significant and private place.

Locating the grave he sought was no problem. While he stood in the exact spot the dead woman's son had also stood in, and gazed from one simple little inexpensive granite slab to the one adjoining it, he tried to remember whatever he had heard of the Beaudrys over the years and had to grudgingly admit that if he had heard anything, it had not been much, and neither had it been anything he could now recall.

It was unsettling, standing there looking at the graves of a man and his wife, both of whom had lived longer than Thad had, up to this time, and had made such a very slight impression upon the world of Almarjal and its countryside that a few years after they had died, people scarcely recalled them except as an obscure pair of people who had not done anything to be remembered for.

A man in his prime felt just very briefly, that cold breath of mortality, and it robbed him of the sense of personal strength, health and durability which had been Thad Mercer's forte ever since middle childhood.

He left the cemetery, finally, walking back in the direction of the lower end of town. At the liverybarn he went out front where the whittlers' bench was, stepped carefully in the presence of the town's old men who had sprayed tobacco juice all around, and did not always look first. He knew each one of them, but in fact there were only three of them at the bench today. Normally there were five or six.

A lined, seamed, wispy man glanced up, toothless jaws rhythmically working, recognised the lawman, spat aside then shifted his cud and said, "Marshal— how be you?"

Thad nodded to all three of them. "Fine, gents. I hope you are the same."

This elicited no reply at all and two of the old men went back to dozing under their tipped-forward hat brims, but the wispy whittler kept crafty, perpetually narrowed, faded eyes upon Mercer. "Y'got somethin' on your mind, Marshal?" he asked, and ceased working his jaws while awaiting the answer.

"A question," responded Thad. "There were some folks named Beaudry lived hereabout some years back. ..."

"Sure did," confirmed the wispy old man, and snapped closed his whittling knife as he said, "You know where that Baptist preacher lived for a few years, until he went back to Texas last spring? Well; that's where the Beaudrys lived. That little acreage north-east of town, just beyond the town-limits where someone painted the trunk of an old cottonwood tree out front with silver paint plumb around and around. Probably was one of them Beaudry kids. Got into one of the old man's paint pots, I'd guess. What was it you wanted to know about them?"

The old man had already given Thad an answer without Thad's question ever being asked: Where had they lived? "Just curious about them," he murmured.

"Someone brought up their name lately and I didn't remember them."

"No reason to remember them," exclaimed the wispy older man. "George—well he was just George the hostler around town. Never done anything much. And Rachel—that was his wife—she taken the lung fever or something like that—I don't remember a lot of things like I used to, for a damned fact, Marshal—anyway she lingered around gettin' scrawnier'n scrawnier'n by the day. George—he was workin' up at the corralyard by then—one day he went home and she was lyin' flat out on their bed sicker'n a dog ... But by gawd you want to know a funny thing? Old George beat her to it after all. Only with him, he just didn't feel real good one day and went home—and hell—he upped and died the same day."

The story-teller leaned to let fly, hauled back upright again and made a little fluttery gesture with both hands. "She didn't hang on much after that. The girl married a dry-goods pedlar out'n Council Bluffs and they went down south somewhere, and the lad, his name was George, he taken up with some cowboys who was heading up north into Wyoming or maybe it was Montana, to commence being a rangerider ... That's the whole darned story, Marshal."

Thad was satisfied it was indeed the whole story and despite the small variations in detail, everyone told it pretty much the same way.

Thad left the old men, walking on a diagonal course to the far side of the roadway, where sunshine was just beginning to reach beneath the warped old plank overhangs as he headed for the little abandoned squatter's place north-east of town which he had ridden past a hundred times without ever before feeling the slightest interest in it. This time, he felt interest, but when he eventually walked out there through weeds and refuse, he was not at all certain why he had made the trip.

He had not expected to encounter George Beaudry here. There was nothing to indicate that anyone had even camped in the slowly deteriorating little shanty for months, but the place had been used, by freighters, itinerant riders moving through, adventuresome lads from town willing to drag some blankets and candles out there and risk the 'haunts' by sleeping beneath a dead old apple tree which had not been cut back in many years. It was still from time to time trying to shelter varieties of wandering humanity.

Pathetically, a broken rope swing dangled from one low limb of a huge, unkempt old cottonwood tree. Nearby where a man had built a stout wooden frame around his dug-well, wet-rot was taking its toll.

Thad found boot marks, had no difficulty imagining who they had belonged to, and stood a while in the haunted hush just looking, listening, and 'feeling', then he turned back towards town, and if he had actually accomplished much by familiarising himself with the grave of the elder Beaudrys, and the crude little poverty-stricken shanty where they had tried to raise their children, he could not pin it down and define it.

He could not even say to himself why he had felt impelled to visit the cemetery, and the pathetic little shanty.

7

MAX AND ERNIE

Max Jeeter had been corralyard foreman for the stage company's Almarjal station for more years than he and a lot of other people cared to think about, and whatever it was that could happen, had at some time during Max's long tenure, happened before.

There were some things Max had witnessed— stages arriving with arrows embedded in their woodwork—which no longer happened, plus a long list of things which sagacity and concern prevented from happening nowadays as often as they had once happened, but not very long after Max and the town marshal had talked about George Beaudry, and neither one had much reason to still be thinking of the other, Max came quietly down the plankwalk, barged into the jailhouse office, bobbed his head to show respect, as he usually did with people, and without raising his voice nor in any other way acting as though what he had to say was upsetting, made an announcement which over the decades he'd had plenty of previous practice at making.

"Marshal, we got a robbed stagecoach up in the corralyard!"

Max's calmness no doubt played its part in Thad

Mercer's reaction to that announcement, but in his own way Thad was a man with a great amount of built-in acceptance of things, and events, so after staring a moment, he leaned to pick up a cigarette he'd been smoking, and said, "Where and when, Max?"

"Early this morning on the north road. About mid-way between town and the north foothills."

Thad looked baffled. "That's all open country."

Max nodded. "Mostly, it's open. He wasn't behind no tree, if that's what you was thinkin', but there's some washouts up through there, and the driver figures, since he never seen the man's horse, he most likely had it hid down in a washout, and most likely the man himself hid out down there until the coach come along."

"Then he walked out and threw down on 'em?" said Thad, still looking a trifle puzzled. "Didn't they see him before they had to haul down?"

"No sir. There was a dead cow in the road. The driver seen that from a half-mile off, but he had to slow to a walk because there's a company policy if a driver's got to wheel off the road on a shoulder or even get plumb off onto the range, he's got to walk his hitch and make darned sure he won't turn over or get stuck or something like that. This feller was at a walk. He was lookin' at the cow, wonderin' how the blasted thing ever happened to just up and drop dead right athwart the roadway—and pulled almost to a stop, fixing to turn off, you see, when this feller with the cocked carbine walks up on his blind side." Max scratched, looked around, and finally said, "That was all there was to it. Except that he taken six hunnert dollars off the passengers, and he taken a mail sack off the coach, plus the driver's gold watch and guns."

Thad reached for his hat. "Where is the driver now?"

"Up yonder at the corralyard. The manager's gone. He went down to Deming day before yestiddy and likely won't be back until about the end of next week. His daughter's gettin' married down there. That leaves me as head In'ian, Marshal. If you want, I'll keep that driver here for a day or two so's you can talk to him."

Thad had no intention of talking to a coach-driver or anyone else for two days so as he headed for the door he said, "Hour ought to be enough, Max. What's his name?"

"Ernest. Ernie Bekins. He's one of our best men. Reliable and never bellyaches."

"Did he have a gunguard with him?"

"Naw; not on a plain everyday passenger run over a route where we ain't been raided in six or seven years. That'd be a plumb waste of money, Marshal."

Maybe the stage company considered it a waste of money, but Max and Thad had not progressed northward towards the corralyard more than a hundred feet before two men, one a hardware pedlar, the other a harness-goods pedlar, came charging towards them bitterly complaining about how the stage-driver had just sat up there, had not done a cussed thing to prevent the pedlars from being robbed. Someone, clearly, would not have considered seeing a gunguard up there beside the driver, a waste of money.

All Thad could tell the salesmen was that the law would do everything possible to find the culprit and

get back their money. The harness-pedlar was an
older man, tough and wise and cynical.

"Nobody ever gets back cash money. Maybe a
watch or a gun or something like a ring or a
necklace—but never any money!"

He stood glowering. Thad had the clear impression
that what the harness-pedlar was thinking had to do
with the possibility that even if Thad did in fact get
their money back, he would forget he'd retrieved it.

There was reason to agree with that logic. Scarcely
a season passed that someone, a constable in some
town or a range detective, or a sheriff or deputy, did
in fact get caught spending a lot more money than
they ever made at their jobs.

But this time Thad gazed at the older pedlar and
said, "If I find the feller before he finds a town and
spends it all, mister, you'll get every darned cent of it
back."

They walked on, found the stagecoach-driver out
back in the autumn sunshine, shaving with his shirt
off, his hat and vest, all piled nearby on the
bunkhouse porch, angling his head so that he could
make a nice long cruise up from his Adam's-apple to
his chin with a wicked-looking bone-handled straight-
razor.

Ernie peered over his shoulder at them from the
cracked bunkhouse mirror, lowered the razor at sight
of Thad's badge, and said, "Sure worked that on me
slick as a damn, Marshal. No pile of tumbleweeds
nor a log, nor boulders, none of them things which
would make a feller curious."

"Yeah," conceded Thad dryly. "Especially out

where there are no rocks nor trees for a couple miles."

Ernie went back to his shaving and for a moment punished the lawman for his sarcasm by shaving and not opening his mouth again. Finally, washing off the blade in the basin in front of him he also said, "Dead cow ... You know, a man just naturally wonders. You know how it is; most of us been rangemen one time or another and we see something like that ..." Ernie flexed both elbows and raised his head to go on shaving. "I just seen the dead critter and was wondering how in hell she ever come to drop dead right smack-dab in the centre of the road. I wasn't thinkin' of nothin' else, and when I heard someone I looked around—by gawd there he was, cocked Winchester and all. I never been so surprised in my life, Marshal, and I been held up a few times before. There he was, by gawd, just like he rose up out of the earth—him and that blasted Winchester ... He lined us up, robbed us, then sent us on our way."

"Like an experienced highwayman," muttered Max Jeeter, and earned a fresh look and head-wag from the driver.

"Well sir, Max, when you come right down to it— that's why none of us said a word nor hesitated when he told us to do something. He was nervous as a cat. He was sweatin' and it wasn't that warm up yonder this morning. Nervous and pale jumpy."

Thad studied Ernie Bekins. "You've been raided before?"

"Yes sir," answered the driver. "I been tooling coaches seventeen years this autumn, and I think I been stopped by highwayman about seven, eight times. If I got to figure, I can come up with the exact number in a few—"

"And this time the man was a greenhorn?"

"Yes, sir. That's sure the feeling us fellers got who was robbed. Me and the passengers talked about it. That man was as jumpy and pale and nervous as a cat."

"What did he look like?"

Ernie turned back to bend down and sluice grey water over his shaved countenance, blew like a whale, then groped for his equally as grey towel as he muttered an answer.

"Looked like an everyday cowboy to me, gents. Tall, maybe about as tall as I am, and skinny. Skinnier'n me and I weigh a hunnert and seventy pounds and am six foot one inch. Not no kid, Marshal, maybe about thirty, grey eyes and sandy hair and looked like his whiskers was maybe a month old or maybe two months old. Needed shearing, so I'd say he'd been somewhere, away from a town for a spell."

"You didn't see his horse nor his outfit?"

"Nope. Just him standin' there when I hauled down to a stop before reining off the roadbed." Ernie turned and reached for his shirt. "There's erosion gullies up in there though, Marshal." Ernie smiled for the first time. He was a tall, thin, sinewy man of indeterminate age, leathery in the face and stone-steady the way he looked at people. "He hit it lucky is all. Normally the most they get off'n passengers is a watch, maybe a finger-ring or a stick-pin if you got town-folks on board, and maybe six or eight dollars. In fact in all the other times I been stopped by

bandits they never even come close to getting that
kind of money. Wouldn't have this time, either, those
pedlars told me, except they was both packin'
advance payments from customers for orders of their
goods." Ernie buttoned his shirt, clapped on his old
hat and looked at Max Jeeter. "I might as well lay
around today, eh?"

Max said, "Why?"

"Well, gawddammit, the marshal'll need to talk a
little more and after all, Max, I just been robbed.
They taken my watch and guns."

With an unsympathetic glare Max said, "Lyin'
around Almarjal isn't going to bring those things
back, Ernie, and anyway, we got a south-bound with
a regular driver down abed with the croup."

"A grown man with the croup?" asked the driver,
giving Max a look of frank disbelief.

"Go ask Doc Hightower if you don't believe me,"
replied Max, and turned as Thad Mercer asked the
driver another question.

"After he had ordered you to drive on—when you
looked back what was he doing?"

"Walking northward back up road as plain as
you could imagine. Walkin' back up there with the
Winchester over his shoulder and carryin' his loot
from the robbery in a red bandanna."

"Towards the foothills?"

Ernie nodded. "Arrow straight for them, Marshal."

Thad let his breath out slowly, then nodded at the
corralyard boss and the driver. "I'm obliged to you
gents," he said, and turned under their solemn gazes

and went walking back out of the corralyard southward in the direction of his office.

Ernie flapped long thin arms like a fledgling big stork. "That's all, by gawd?"

Max acted knowledgeable. "What else did you expect?"

"Well ... I dunno ... but after all I been robbed and my passengers was cleaned out and all."

Max spat, then jerked his head. "Come on inside the office. I know where the manager hides his whisky. You got that much coming anyway."

Ernie looked monumentally disgusted. "A lousy gawddamned shot of whisky an' I just been lookin' right down the gunbarrel of a murderin' darned highwayman. For that I get one lousy shot of whisky!"

Max was a pragmatic individual. "It could have been worse, Ernie. If you'd bobbled and the bastard had shot you—right now you wouldn't even be gettin' any whisky."

Ernie turned thoughtful as they entered the front office. "I don't know," he murmured. "I tried to make up my mind about that on the ride down here. Would that feller have shot, or wouldn't he have?"

Max was peering into a cupboard as he said, "If you'd got to fooling around you'd have found out. And if he was one of those highwaymen who do ... Here it is! Look at this. Bonded whisky from Philadelphia."

Ernie did indeed look. "Bonded—pure stuff by gawd. I didn't know his job paid that good. Hey; if you pour two full glasses of that stuff, Max, he's goin' to know it, ain't he?"

"Naw. I been taking a nip now and then for years and he's never suspected anything yet. Because I fill the bottle back up again with water."

"Jesus! You'd pour water into this kind of whisky?"

"It's better'n getting fired!"

The driver accepted a glass, tasted it, and smacked his lips as though he were an experienced whisky-drinker, which he was not, but even so the kind of whisky he was sampling now was so noticeably smooth and mellow he did not have to be an authority to appreciate it. Then he tasted it several more times and said, "This here is the best likker I ever drank, Max." He held the glass aloft to catch sunlight through it. "Something I didn't tell the lawman," he said, still squinting at sunlight through his whisky. "It probably didn't mean anything anyhow."

"What didn't?"

"I wasn't sure of it. That's why I never mentioned it." Ernie swilled down more of his whisky, softly belched and turned a very benign look upon Max Jeeter as he said, "It didn't seem to me that highway-man was really alone."

"You said—you told the constable—"

"I know. And that's why I never told him other-wise. The feller showed up by hisself, robbed us by hisself and went walkin' northward back up into the foothills by hisself, but twice when he was robbin' us he'd turn quick-like and peer off through the north-westerly grass and underbrush. Twice he did that. Like maybe he wanted to be sure someone who was maybe lying on their belly out there was watching— or something. Then, when he went walkin' up the road after he'd cleaned us of our money and guns and all, he kept lookin' over in that same direction. So I just naturally got a feeling ... How about another half-glass of the whisky?"

Max dutifully leaned to pour, watching the level of amber liquid in the glass get steadily lower. There was a point, of course, beyond which you could not add water or the taste would be ruined and the deception would be easily discovered.

Still—what the hell—the manager had three more of those bottles cached away behind all the papers in that cupboard.

Max poured a half-glass more for Ernie, then treated himself to another half-glass, and there was one charming element about that kind of superior whisky—it could fix a man so's he couldn't reach around and find his butt with both hands, after the second glass, but the effect was slow to arrive. In fact, Max was back out in the yard supervising some repair work on one of the coaches, and Ernie had gone over to the corralyard bunkhouse to put away his shaving equipment, before the full force finally crept up and assaulted them both.

8

HUNCHES

This time the tracks were clear and uncluttered as Thad walked his horse out westerly from where that dead cow was lying.

The highwayman had come forward alone, but back where he had been lying in the grass there was plenty of sign that he had not been alone at all, that two other men had sat back there with him.

All three of them had smoked cigarettes, had left the ruptured butts in the grass, where they had also left pressed-down grass where more than one man had sat or hunkered, and Thad did not follow the single set of bootmarks which went toward the roadway, he turned back and followed the second pair of tracks which left the hiding-place in the grass and went north-westerly into the lower cuts and bays where the foothills began.

He dismounted back up in there, tied his animal in tree shade and went the balance of the distance on foot.

Three animals had been tethered behind the low, thick shoulder of a hillock near a thicket of chaparral. Judging from the mounded droppings those three horses had stood back in there out of sight of the roadway for most of the early morning.

Thad smoked, threw down the butt and swore. He was not a good enough mathematician so he had to pick up a twig, smooth off some ground and add it up in the dust.

Three thousand dollars from the bank, for those three, then twenty-five hundred from old Billings, the next time they raided, and now six hundred from the stage—which was not counting the driver's watch and guns, and whatever else they had taken from the passengers. In money alone, then, those three sons of bitches had made sixty-one hundred darned dollars, and they had managed to make those wages in something like a week.

He threw down the stick, scuffed out his numerals and stood up to start walking out and around in order to see what else he might turn up.

When they had ridden away from the place where their animals had patiently waited, the trio had gone due west in and out along the base of the foothills. Thad did not walk after them for more than a mile. He turned back, found his horse sound asleep when he got back to the tree-shade, and instead of untying and riding off, perhaps to take up the cold trail, he sat down at the base of the tree, leaned back and pondered what had been a suspicion before he had got out here, and which was now almost a complete certainty.

Those same three bastards again! Maybe one was named George Beaudry. There was a right good chance his name was Beaudry.

If this third raid had done anything for Thad

Mercer it was to furnish him with the third description. The third rangeman was tall and lean and grey-eyed and sandy-haired—and whiskery. All three of them were whiskery, all three of them looked as though they had not been near a barber in a long while, nor had been either willing or able to shave for a long while.

That did in fact sound pretty much like Ernie Bekins's supposition: men who had not been near a town for a long while. They could of course be pothunters fresh down from a season of jerking meat in the back-country, or it could be a trio of rangeriders who had decided turning outlaw was a better way to make a living than range-riding. Well; a man would not get much of an argument about that; six thousand and one hundred dollars split three ways among men who had probably never before made more than twelve dollars a month in their entire misbegotten lives, and had made all that loot in less than one week. ...

Thad's horse opened one eye, then the other, gazed without noticeable like nor dislike at the man seated in speckled shade nearby, then raised his head higher, turned and looked back in the direction of the roadway where that dead cow was gently swelling.

Thad got to his feet, also considered the cow, decided that Max would not do it, no one else would do it, so he might as well. Taking up some slack in his cincha before swinging across leather, Thad took down his lariat, shook out a careless little loop—this old cow was not going to duck and weave—dropped his toss directly over the head, gave it a couple of flips to get both horns inside the loop, then took up his slack, turned, and the horse had to strain, hump up and grunt because the old cow also weighed quite a bit. The horse did not beat her by more than about two hundred pounds and the old cow weighed an easy eight hundred.

Nor did she co-operate one blasted bit. It was like moving nearly a half ton of lead, but once the horse broke her loose, got her moving, he dug in and kept the initiative until she was about a hundred yards from the roadway, and by then the horse was breathing hard so Thad slacked off, stepped down to free his rope—and found the small bullet hole as neat as a dark little pencil-mark in the whorl of white hair directly between and slightly above, the dead eyes.

Someone had shot that cow up close. Probably after she had been roped and the assassin could get down and walk up, gun extended, while one of the other ones, or maybe both the other men, held the cow still. It would then be very easy for three horses to drag her over into place in the roadway.

It was a JB cow. When John Billings found all this out he was going to be as mad as a wet hen, all over again.

Thad stood, loosening the cincha until his horse had had his blow, and speculating whether or not this dead cow might have been part of that little bunch those men had driven across the bank-robber's tracks. She was a little more northward from where Thad had found those other cows, but if the trio of renegades had decided to rob the stage that far in advance of when they had actually done it, they could very easily have cut her out and choused her up here.

Of course—if those men had done something like

this, then they had also known when that stagecoach was due, and again, that indicated to Thad Mercer that either one of them or perhaps all of them, were a lot more familiar with customs and events and people around the Almarjal countryside than bandits normally were.

He finished coiling his rope, secured it to the swells, let his horse drag the reins and graze along for a short distance while Thad stood gazing over at that bloating big old redback cow, and began to think back to the three descriptions he now had.

Of course he could be jumping to a conclusion this time. There was actually nothing—no real proof at all—to support his hunch that this was the same trio of rangemen who had committed those other crimes.

Except that he was entirely satisfied, deep down, that this was exactly who they were. And now he was beginning to form an additional opinion: they were not professionals. If they had indeed committed robberies before, for a fact at least this one of them had not committed very many, and probably none of them had, because in each instance there had been something—a nervous look around, a fixed, death's-head grin, or a sweating face and hands—to indicate that none of them were very hardened at what they were now engaged in.

He walked along with his horse for a while, paralleling the roadway and enjoying the late-day warmth, considering the trio of outlaws he was privately involved with. In fact he walked almost a mile and a half before mounting to continue on the rest of the way to town, where he arrived at red sunset, with the roadway practically empty and most of the stores either closed up for the day or about to be closed up.

He left his horse with the liveryman hostler and ambled back to his office thinking that he probably should make a more painstaking search among the dodgers; if those three were experienced at all, even with only one or two previous robberies to their credit, at least one of them would possibly have a dodger out on him.

He did not get the chance to make that search, nor did it trouble him very much that he didn't. When he shoved open the door Old Man Billings was sitting at a chair, tilted back along the north wall, as though he were a permanent fixture in the jailhouse office.

He did not greet the constable. Instead, he gruffly said, "Don't bother telling me, I already know. It's a JB cow."

Evidently the news of that coach robbery had been passed around town already. No reason of course for it not to be, and since there were two windy pedlars plus a stage-driver to talk about it ... "Yeah, it was one of yours. Nice big cow, but got a little age on her. Who told you?" Thad asked, going over to the desk to pitch aside his hat and drop into a chair.

"Some fellers at the saloon, but they were late. After you kept askin' about some of the cattle being moved from the east range over across the stageroad, I sent some boys out there. They found her in the centre of the road. Shot dead and dragged. I came to town to tell you, stopped to have some beer, and heard the whole story at the bar." Billings put his shrewd eyes upon the lawman. "Well. ...?"

"Well what? You lost a cow. They shot her,

dragged her into the road to stop the coach, robbed it, got something like six hundred dollars, and ran for it."

Billings's shrewd look deepened, his crafty old faded eyes were like steel marbles. "They?" he asked. "Everyone at the saloon said it was one highwayman. One feller on foot who crept out of the grass, or something like that."

Thad swore under his breath. That had been a slip of the tongue purely and simply. He shrugged and leaned forward on the desk.

"Same three, Mister Billings."

"What!"

Thad went over to rattle the coffeepot. It was empty and he did not really want any coffee badly enough to stoke up a fire, and make a fresh pot-load too, so he spoke as he returned to the desk.

"One of them stopped the stage, but there were two more lyin' back. They had horses tethered up behind a knoll." Thad met the cowman's stare easily. "I don't have very much proof. What I've got is the tracks of three men up there, three hidden horses, two other men lyin' back and after the robbery three horsemen joining together to ride westerly. Not anything you could use in a court of law."

"Court of law my butt," exclaimed the cowman. "Those sons of bitches aren't going to see the inside of any law court—if I can prevent it! Westerly from where they stopped the stage, you say?"

Thad nodded. "Do you think three men who have planned all this as well as those fellers have, didn't also figure you—or me—or a posse, or someone anyway, would try to run them down by their tracks?

Sure; they went west against the foothills and if you go up there and go hootin' and hollerin' in pursuit you're going to get a surprise. Those men won't be at the end of the trail, when you ride your duff off trying to find them."

Billings appeared to accept this, but of course not with any show of good grace as he said, "All right; how do we do it then?"

"*We* don't, Mister Billings. *I* do."

"You just told me how clever and all they are. You think you can find them alone and come out of it still breathing?"

"Maybe not. I'm sure as hell not going to scuff up any big dust-cloud leading you and your riders in a manhunt, either. Not with those men watching."

"Hell," scoffed Billings, "they won't still be in the country."

"They hung around after they raided the bank, and then raided you didn't they?"

"Sure. But unless they are plumb fools after this latest raid they'll know better. Even if they are just common-place rangeriders, they'll be *that* smart." Billings bobbed his head as though to emphasise what he had just said, then, for a moment, he continued to just sit and gaze across in the direction of the desk before finally arising with a little stiff effort, and to say, "Damnedest thing I ever ran across," and went over to the door to lean there and look back.

Thad made a gesture. "What's so hard to believe about it? Whoever they are, sure as hell they know this country, and a whole lot more. If I was going to take up their line of work I'd want to do it about the same—"

"Not *that*," exclaimed old Billings, opening the door to pass on outside. "How you figured them out—*that's* the damnedest thing I ever run across."

He closed the door, and Thad, who had intended to ask him what disposal he meant to make of that dead cow up yonder, did not get a chance to ask.

He had a fair idea. Billings would do nothing. There were bones scattered all across every big cow range where animals had died, and had been left to themselves with scrupulous disregard by both ranchers and rangeriders. All that could be done anyway, was send a wagon over there with several big tins of coal oil and burn the carcass, and that was expensive, time-consuming, and darned unpleasant.

On the other hand, that close to the roadway ... Thad grabbed his hat and went down to the livery-barn in search of the proprietor of the place. When he found him—out back at the wash-rack with a magnificent team of matched Belgians, both sorrels with flaxen manes and tails—he said, "You heard about the coach-robbery, did you?" and as soon as the liveryman assented, then broadly smiled over the way that highwayman had stopped the stage, Thad returned his broad smile with one just as broad as he said, "You can take a team up there, Alex, and tie onto that cow carcass before it gets any fresher, and drag it a mile or so off. It would be a real fine example of you showin' your civic spirit."

The liveryman was no longer smiling by the time Thad had finished. "What civic spirit?" he demanded in a gravelly voice. "Don't I donate the use of a wagon for the school's annual hayride each summer, and—."

"Alex; that cow is only as far off the road as my saddlehorse could snake her. She's too hefty for an average saddlehorse to pull around."

"Who pays me, Thad? You see this team? You got any notion how much they cost to buy—and by the Lord you never seen horses that could *eat* like this pair."

"I'll take it up the very next time the Town Council sits, Alex."

The liveryman snorted. "They ain't paid me yet for that dead bear some idiot shot in the west alleyway when he come outside in the night to pee, and seen the bear rummaging the trash barrels." Alex snorted again. "By grabs, Thad, that there happened three years ago!"

"All right, then. I'll pay you. But we got to get her dragged away from the road before she swells up and—."

"Don't she belong to John Billings?"

"Yeah. When she was standing up and eating grass she did, but you know those cowmen never look twice at a dead one."

The liveryman groaned, rolled up his eyes, assumed a look of beatific martyrdom, then lowered his eyes to Thad Mercer and said, "And if I do it— the next time one of my hostlers gets smoked up and I need him down here. ...?"

Thad was perfectly agreeable. "I won't lock him up. Or if I have to lock him up, I'll turn him over to you the very next morning. Are you going to take a chain and a team and go up there?"

"Yas, yas gawddammit I'll go. Thad, if you'd been

borned a woman you'd have been the naggingest old witch in the territory!"

Thad smiled. "When you get back come by the saloon and I'll stand the drinks."

"Well," mumbled the crestfallen liveryman, "at least *that* much I can agree with you about!"

9

AQUA FRIO

The morning after the stagecoach robbery Thad Mercer awakened with more than just a stale-whisky taste in his mouth, he sat up to blearily gaze out into the empty roadway, scratch, and face one of those disconcerting thoughts which occasionally were in a man's mind when he first awakened in the morning.

Those three outlaws would strike again as sure as the Good Lord had made little green apples. Not only that, but since the other two had made successful raids which had netted them loot into the thousands, that lanky one who had stopped the coach and who had only come away with six hundred dollars, would probably feel a very strong motivation to try and do better—next time.

Thad considered only the bad aspects of this until he got down to the cafe, one of the first customers of the pre-dawn morning. After a hot cup of black java he began to speculate on where, exactly, those men would strike again, for their fourth time.

Almarjal was an excellent possibility. As a general rule the only two places in cow country where outlaws could find large amounts of cash money readily at hand were in towns, or out somewhere on a big cow outfit—like JB, for example—but by the time Thad's breakfast arrived, he had come to a conclusion about raiding those cow outfits: after what had happened to Billings, and after news of that happening had spread far and wide over the ranges, one stranger or a trio of them approaching a cow outfit, except in the pit of the night, would certainly be watched intently. And even if they tried it in the late night as they had done so successfully at JB, there was a fine chance that all the outfits now were ready and waiting.

As for stagecoaches, even if they found another one with six hundred dollars among its passengers, and they'd surely not expect such a windfall twice in a row, it just was not the kind of money they had become accustomed to looting, after the JB and bank robberies.

Thad finished breakfast, got more coffee, sat there rolling a smoke to go with his fresh cup of java, and decided that although he could imagine where they might strike again, he could also think of many reasons why they might not care to do any of those things, and that left him just about where he had been last night when he'd got back to town.

The cafeman came along to mop sweat—it was hot in his windowless little cubbyhole of a kitchen even this early in the morning—and to gaze speculatively at the lawman's troubled countenance as he said, "This here darned countryside is sure gettin' full of renegades all of a sudden, Marshal. The bank, old JB, and a stagecoach. Next thing one of 'em'll walk in here and level his pistol at me."

Thad looked up. They would not even get six

hundred in here. He said, "All they'd get is indigestion."

The cafeman smiled but it took real effort. Not that he could not take a little joshing, he could, except that right now it was a little early in the day. The sun wasn't even out yet.

Thad left after his second cup of coffee, ambled over to open his office for the day, turned to watch a special stagecoach come up from the south, and while he was wondering about that, someone down at the liverybarn let out a loud squawk, then followed this with a string of heartfelt profanity.

There were few places in town where accidents, deliberate and otherwise, happened with the frequency that obtained around a liverybarn. A man did not have to get kicked, nor even bitten, although those things occurred often enough, he could get stepped on, for example, and there was no more excruciating agony than to have a thousand-pound saddle animal with steel shoes on his hooves, step squarely upon a man's foot.

Or it could have been a knock-down; that too was part of the hazard. Thad shrugged and went inside, turned to watch as that southern coach went past at a jangling walk, caught sight of a handsome woman inside the stage, along with three other passengers, all male, and idly wondered what the handsome woman in her pearl-grey, pert little hat and her pearly-grey coat and gloves, was doing in Almarjal, where about the only time anyone wore gloves, male or female, was when the preacher buried someone and held up the Good Book. He always wore white gloves. It looked solemn, and dignified as all hell.

One of the old gaffers who whiled away his days in tree-shade out front of the liverybarn, on the whittlers' bench down there, came ambling past.

Thad knew him. Everyone in town and two-thirds of the folks—especially the older folks—out over the countryside knew old Jason Beal. He had been a buffalo hunter, an army scout, a freighter, mustanger, rangerider, whatever a man had been required to do to survive years back, old Jase Beal had become proficient at it. There were ancient rumours that some of the things old Jason Beal had done, forty years earlier, were things men could no longer do without an excellent chance that they would be hanged for doing them.

Jason Beal was the only man around the Almarjal countryside who could recall John Billings as a young man. Thad had heard Jase one time, up at the saloon, and what he had said had not been calculated to glorify Billings.

But Thad Mercer had few illusions. Also, he was a fair judge of male humanity; an old man like Billings who was mean when he had to be even at his age, could be expected to have been a lot meaner when he'd been at that yeasty time of life.

Jase peered in through the open jailhouse door, paused as he saw movement in the gloom, and leaned for a better stare. Then he said, "Good morning, Marshal. That was interestin' that coach-robbery up the road a-ways yestiddy, wasn't it?"

Thad could not hold back a bitter little grin when he replied. "Interesting isn't the word I'd use to describe it, Jase ... Care for some coffee? I was about to set a fresh pot on to boil."

Old Beal walked in. He was a wiry, shrunken old man the colour of harness leather which had been oiled and left in the sun. His eyes had once been intensely blue, now they had an opaque cast to them and were more nearly grey. In fact it was Jase Beal's eyes which were just now beginning to go. The rest of him remained as stringy, spare and sinewy as an old length of rawhide.

He avoided the chairs and sought a place along the back-wall bench as he said, "That warn't the place where most stages been stopped over the years, Marshal. I'd say he was a greenhorn to stop one out where there warn't no cover if the driver or a passenger decided to chouse him." Jase sat down, peered at his scuffed, cracked boots and pulled both feet far back under the bench where the most obvious proof of his poverty would not show.

Thad finished at the stove and went over to his desk. An idea had occurred to him when he'd seen old Beal coming down the plankwalk. He fished for his makings as he sat down, and said, "Out pretty early, aren't you, Jase?"

"Well yas; my daughter-in-law ... she's a fine person, you understand. A man couldn't ask for a woman who looks after his son better and keeps a short rein on them half-growed sons of hers any better ... Well; it's just—I guess—too many years between us, Marshal."

Thad nodded solemnly and did not pursue this topic. He knew old Jase's son—who had buttermilk for a backbone—and he knew the daughter-in-law. She was a buxom, muscular, big dark-eyed Texan as thick as an oak and positive in everything she did or said.

He reverted to the hunch he'd had when he'd first spied old Jase hiking southward. "You remember a family named Beaudry who used to live on that tumble-down claim north-east of town a half mile or so, Jase?"

The old man forgot about his cracked boots and shoved both thin legs straight out as he leaned back broadly smiling. "Remember 'em? Why gawddam-mit, sonny, it was me helped Beaudry get established here in town. Got him his first job at the liverybarn. Yeah, I remember 'em." He sobered a little. "Yeah ... it was me pitched in the first handful of dirt on 'em both. On Rachel—she died last. Lord, Marshal, when they first come here she was pretty as a speckled pony. Frail and a little timid and all—but Lord she was somethin' for a man to feast his eyes on ... Died. Died young, and it was a pure pity."

Thad listened. Each time the Beaudrys came up, he learned something else about them. He had heard Rachel Beaudry was frail, before, even sickly, but he'd never before heard that she was also pretty.

"You remember the lad, Jase?"

"Young George? I'd ought to remember him. I used to take him into the hills when I'd go pothun-ting. You see, years back, mostly folks didn't like to leave the settlements. Indians y'see. And for fellers like me who did pothuntin' for a living, well, we kept things going a little." Jase winked slyly. "Wasn't no Indians back up there two-thirds of the time or hell, we wouldn't have been up there neither, but that way we kept folks from tryin' to shoot meat for themselves. A man who is in business for hisself, he's got to be thinkin' all the time, Marshal. You understand?"

Thad 'understood'. He also understood that Jase strayed, so he mentioned the lad again, and Jase picked up the conversation where he'd abandoned it.

"Used to take young George with me now and then. He was a little tyke, dark as a 'breed, and quick as a snake. He could learn fast and do right, and remember well. Him and me got to be real partners. Well, his paw was busy from dawn until dark. It wasn't as simple to keep a job them days as it is now. And Rachel—poor little thing—she was commencing to fail a little even then. Well; I taken young George into the mountains and when he got so's he could shoot straight, I commenced divvying up what we'd get for the meat he downed. First job he ever had." Jason smiled.

The coffee began to boil. Thad allowed it to do this for five minutes then went over and drew off two cups. It was too hot to drink but it smelled wonderful. Jason put his cup on the bench and tested it now and then with an impervious fingertip.

"The lad left here even before his maw passed on. Him and the girl. She got married and went out to San Francisco, I think. George, he taken off one springtime with some loud-talkin' Texans bound up north to Montana or Wyoming. He come down to see me the evening before he left ... Sure did hate to see him go, Marshal. You know, sometimes your own son isn't all—well—he's different from what you'd figured he'd grow up to be, and the lad you accidentally partner up with turns out to be more nearly what you'd had in mind. George was—just one hell of a handy youngster; learnt quick, was tough—bad weather never bothered him—had a cool head on his shoulders ... I said if he'd stay maybe come autumn we could run some trap lines and make ourselves a real stake. Furs was sellin' good back a few years."

"But he didn't stay?"

Jase shook his head. "He didn't stay. Marshal, when you're young the horizon beckons. You know how that is?"

"Yes, I know, Jase. Did you ever see George Beaudry afterwards?"

"Nope, never did. Heard about him a time or two though. He was working the Montana ranges, was a good hand and had learnt the rangeman's trade well. Someday he'll come back. Mostly, folks do that, you know, come back someday and see what things was *really* like where they grew up ... I hope I'm still above the ground, for I'd like to see the lad again. For a damned fact, Marshal." Jase smiled, his milky eyes lifting a little and going far out, and far back.

"Did I ever tell you about the time he played a hell of a prank on me?"

Thad shook his head. Not only hadn't old Jase mentioned this prank but he had never before even mentioned young Beaudry to Thad.

"Well sir, we had a main-camp back a couple miles west of the stage road, and up into the mountains just beyond the foothills at a spring called *Aqua Frio*. We'd usually set up camp there, then make sashays in all directions but mostly northward into the mountains, from our main-camp. Not too much water in them mountains, Marshal. Well, anyway, I used to warn George; I'd tell him not to take food into his bedroll to chew on while he was waitin' to go to sleep. I guess maybe I harped on that a lot. One time I was sound asleep, y'see, and somethin' commenced rollin' me a little from side to side. It woken me up, damn it, and I liked to have heart failure. It was a brown bear. In the dark, me half asleep and all, he looked big enough to throw a saddle on. He got a little mad, finally, and give me a pretty hefty whack, rolled the bedroll with me in it over and over, then he sat down and picked up a chunk of salt pork. Sat right there on his broad behind and whimpered and groaned while he ate that chunk of salt pork."

Jase brought his eyes down to Thad's face. "You know where that blasted kid was? Up a tree about fifty yards away snickering until I thought he'd fall out'n the damned tree. You know what he'd done?"

Thad could guess. "Put that piece of salt pork under your bedroll before you fellers rolled in?"

"Well hell, more'n that, the little shaggy-headed scoundrel. He taken that piece of salt pork, tied a string to it and dragged it all over beyond camp so's some darned varmint would pick up the scent!"

"A bear?" asked Thad, smiling.

"Afterwards, when I could chum him down out'n that blasted tree he said not. Said he figured it'd be a wolf or maybe some coyotes. ... Darned imp, I told him then and there, a man does something like that, and he'd better figure prowling bears will pick up the scent. Not the pork; blasted bear can kill meat any time he's a mind to. The *salt*; they'll do a lot more'n roll a man around in his bedroll like he was a raccoon, to get at a salt lick."

Thad laughed. After a few moments the old man also laughed. He waggled his head. "Yes sir, he was one hell of a lad. And you know, after he left a few years back—well—I only went back up there one more season, then I quit. Gettin' too old I said to my daughter-in-law. T'tell you the truth, Marshal, it just wasn't no fun any more."

Jason Beal picked up the cup and drained it of black coffee. He afterwards smacked his lips. "Had no idea you made such a decent cup of coffee, Marshal, or sure's hell I'd have included you in my morning rounds." He arose and took the cup over to the stove and set it aside.

Thad said, "Come by any morning, Jase. It's not always as fresh as this coffee, but it'll be just as darned hot." He went out to the plankwalk with the old man. The sun was shining now, the town was coming to life, and up at the corralyard that special coach was parked in the gateway, which was unusual, they usually either pulled all the way inside, or they parked out front.

Old Beal sniffled, ran a filthy old coat sleeve under his droopy nose, and used that same arm to toss Thad a salute with, as he turned southward to resume his way down to the whittlers' bench. The reason he was out so early was elemental: the gaffer who got the upper end of the bench first, had warm sunshine on him until the day was warm all over, and while that was nothing of great moment or concern to most folks around town, to the handful of scraggly old scarecrows who came up there each morning, it was the most important event of the entire day.

Thad went back to finish his coffee and to roll a smoke and stand a while in thought. Finally, he finished the java, crushed out his smoke and headed over in the direction of the general store, except that he did not enter there but went past and on up to the gunshop where a greying man about Thad's own age was cursing at a reluctant iron wood-stove because the blasted thing would not draw properly.

The reason was obvious. That lower wide iron door was so fully blocked by ashes there was no draught inside the stove. Thad leaned, watched and listened for a moment, then said, "Al, if you'd clean out the ashes once in a while it'd work."

The gunsmith turned, shot Thad a mean look, then rolled up his eyes. "I hate to clean this blasted thing. Every time I do, dust as thick as sliced bread settles all over everything and I got to spend another hour using the turkey-feather duster."

Thad was not very sympathetic. "This is autumn, Al. The cold weather hasn't even come yet, but it sure as hell will. You don't want to go into the winter with a plugged up stove do you?"

The gunsmith reluctantly began untying his soiled, oily old apron. "You sound just like my wife," he complained. He raised his voice and mimicked her by saying, "Al; why don't you ever clean that stove? You'd ought to be ashamed of yourself!"

Thad Mercer laughed and straightened up off the counter. "Do you know where *Aqua Frio* spring is back in the mountains?" Al turned, apron in hand. "Yes. What's that got to do with this blasted stove?"

"Nothing, as far as I know," stated the town marshal. "I've heard of it a hundred times over the past six or eight years, but I've never been up there. How would a man reach it?"

The gunsmith was a burly, solid, oaken man. He went across to put his apron atop the counter, then he leaned with a sceptical look and said, "It's the wrong time of year to shoot anything, Thad. Bucks are mostly in the velvet and the old boar-bears'll be fixing to den up and all. What the hell do you want to go up there for?"

Thad sighed. "To get away from nosy folks who always got to pry into my business."

Al reddened. "So you expect me to tell you how to get up there?"

"I do."

Al looked unhappy. "I don't know how to explain it to someone who's never been up there."

"Well, damn it all, if I'd been there why would I be in here askin' you how to get there?" demanded Thad, and the gunsmith winced before he answered. "Tell you what; I'll *take* you up there. We could go right now, this morning, and if we make good enough time we'd be back in town this evening. Maybe."

Thad looked at the stove. "You got work to do, Al."

"It can wait. Anyway, I been in here with my beak on the grindstone for two steady months now and I'm due to head out for a few hours. Well ... Marshal?"

Thad kept staring at the stove. Eventually he said, "Not this morning, Al. Late this afternoon."

Al scowled. "Late this afternoon? You got any idea how far it is up there, and back? If we didn't ride out until this afternoon, Thad, we wouldn't be able to get back until before dawn tomorrow, maybe."

The lawman said, "That's right. We probably wouldn't." He stood gazing at the burly gunsmith until the gunsmith's face very slowly assumed a different expression.

Al said, "You got something connected with the law in the back of your mind?"

"Sure have. I don't want anyone to see us riding out of here this morning, and heading up in that direction, Al. What I want is someone along who can find that campsite in the dark if he has to."

"Hmmmmm. You mind telling me what this is about?"

"No. Not after we're out of town this evening. Then I'll tell you the whole story. If you really want to take me up there, but I'd settle for a good description on how to find it by myself."

The gunsmith was positive about one thing. "Not in the dark you couldn't. Not if you need a map to find it in broad daylight ... All right, I'll be ready this evening. You just come by when you figure it's time to head out."

"Al; what about your wife?"

The gunsmith hung fire momentarily, then said, "You leave that to me. One thing marriage does for a man—sure teaches him to be a convincin' liar!"

10

THE WOMAN

Blaine Harper saw the constable leaving Al Trent's gunshop from his window across at the bank, and muttered to himself. He was still not satisfied the lawman was doing what should be done to catch that man who had robbed the bank. John Billings had unceremoniously told him Mercer was doing plenty, and had let it go at that, which was the main reason Blaine did not rush forth now and harass the marshal. Billings was still one of the major controllers of the bank. Also, Blaine Harper had known the old man long enough to be convinced that when he said a man was doing plenty, then that was indeed a fact.

Except that Harper would be damned if he could see how being in town all the time instead of rooting out along someone's back-trail could be considered as 'doing plenty'.

This attitude was not exclusive to the banker. Walt Winters at the store had already mildly complained of something similar, to his clerk. And there were others around town who felt the same way, but when Thad returned to his office he encountered two people who, however they might have been inclined to consider him as a lawman—and it would have to have been an opinion formed from hearsay alone since neither of them had ever set eyes upon Thad Mercer before—had not come to Almarjal to be reproachful or sceptical.

It was that handsome female Thad had glimpsed when that special coach had passed along earlier. The man could have been in there too, but Thad did not remember him. Still, he was not a cowman, and Thad vaguely recalled that one of those male passengers had been wearing a curly-brimmed handsome little derby hat, exactly as this man was wearing.

The man introduced them. He was, he said, Norman Haines and the lady with him was Betsy Haines, his sister. What Norman Haines wanted to know was whether Marshal Mercer knew anything about the Red Rock cattle ranch and range southeast of Almarjal, which had belonged to an old man named Sunday, Reg Sunday.

Thad compelled himself to concentrate upon the man even though he could feel the woman's very dark, brilliant eyes fully upon him. It was as though they had known one another, as though in fact they had known one another very well and in her presence Thad had difficulty thinking of other things. He had to make an effort, as now when he answered the man.

"Yes, I know the Red Rock country—and knew Mister Sunday fairly well. He's been dead now about four years. I helped his folks, from Cincinnati, when they came out here to liquidate everything."

"Well," stated Norman Haines, "we are also from Cincinnati, and we bought the ranch and its range-rights from Reg Sunday's heirs." Haines smiled. He was a handsome man, tanned and fit-looking. Once

he shed those button shoes, that fancy little curly-
brimmed hat and those peg-top pants with the
tight-fitting pretty damned useless jacket which
matched the britches, and got into something more
fitting, he could pass as a cowman. He was tall, about
Thad's height, and broad-shouldered and lean-
flanked. Not everyone who came out, made it, but
this was the kind of a man who would if anyone
would.

Thad turned slowly, braced and ready for the
dead-level liquid dark gaze from the handsome
woman. She faintly smiled at him. He smiled back,
then turned to go behind his desk and to offer them
chairs. "You arrived on the special stage," he said,
matter-of-factly, and passed over that quickly by also
saying, "We don't see enough of 'em not to pay
attention when one comes through."

Haines smiled as he sat beside the handsome
dark-eyed woman on the wall-bench. "It wasn't our
coach, Constable. We didn't charter it. Those other
two passengers were carrying light freight on through
up north to a place called Cinnebar where they had a
mine. They chartered it and we were just lucky
enough to be taken aboard down at Tucumcari. Now
about the Red Rock ranch ..."

Thad's glance drifted back to the very handsome
woman. She was tall for a female, maybe as much as
five feet and five or six inches, but she had been fed
up by someone like a pure-bred heifer until the meat
spread around over that tall framework had been
magnificently distributed. When she looked back at
him, with that hint of a faint smile he could feel the
tug as though they had been lovers of long standing.

It had never before happened to him, exactly like that.

"It's a big outfit," he answered the man while looking directly at Betsy. "Got good water, which is important here—or anywhere, I guess, Mister Haines—and the buildings are pretty run-down now, after no one living out there for the past few years, but they're solid."

"Neighbours, Constable?"

Thad rubbed his jaw. "John Billings on three sides of you. He's the biggest range cowman around the Almarjal countryside."

"Young, is he?"

"No sir, he's old."

"Friendly, is he?"

Thad reluctantly swung his glance back to Norman Haines now. "Well; he's honest and he's fair."

The beautiful woman laughed quietly. "Hard old shellback, Mister Mercer?"

Thad welcomed the chance to smile at her. It was like letting go some rough and pent-up emotion. "That could be a fair description, Miss Haines. Right now he's not likely to welcome newcomers. He's been having a little trouble lately."

The warm dark eyes never left Thad's face. "Would he welcome newcomers any time, Constable?"

Thad's smile deepened a trifle. "Likely not, ma'am. In this country the folks who've been around longest don't like to see newcomers arrive. I think it's like that everywhere, though. Do you folks figure to ranch the Red Rock place?"

The woman nodded. "Yes. That's why we bought it. But we're total strangers."

Thad ignored the little warning in his mind and said, "If you need a friend out here, Miss Haines, you got one right now and from here on."

Her brother cleared his throat. "We don't want to take up too much of your time, Constable. You are no doubt a busy man." He got to his feet. "Incidentally, it's Mistress not Miss Haines." He offered a hand which Thad arose to grasp, and to immediately release as he moved to the door to hold it open for them.

The handsome woman walked out last, paused for a moment to look Thad Mercer squarely in the eye as she said, "*Mistress* Haines, Constable. I am a widow." She turned and leaned slightly to glance northward. "Do they take strangers in up at the hotel?"

He lifted his glance from her profile slowly. "Yes'm. It's really a boarding-house. I live up there." He immediately said, "So do a lot of the single folks around town."

She stepped out upon the plankwalk. "We are obliged for your help, Constable—and for your friendliness."

Thad remained rooted in the doorway watching them walk away. When the gunsmith came strolling along moments later, without his apron and wearing a hat for a change, he looked up, looked up again, then said, "What's bothering you?"

Mercer answered honestly. "You see those folks up yonder on the east side of the road by the boarding-house porch?"

Al Trent turned. "You mean the city-ones? Yeah, I see them—what of it?"

"I never saw a woman like that up close before in my life," stated the lawman, and Al turned back slowly, his thick body slack as he screwed up his face.

"Just a woman, Marshal. They come in all sizes and shapes but hell they're all just female-women."

"Not that one, Al."

Trent swung for another look but they had disappeared inside the boarding-house so he shrugged powerful shoulders and resettled the hat which he was unaccustomed to wearing, and said, "Let me tell you something I know from bein' married eleven years: some of 'em cook better'n others, some got better builds, some are fair or dark or in-between, but Thad, after six or eight years of bein' married to one of them they all commence to sound the same, for a darned fact. I know; I just come from tellin' mine I wouldn't be home for supper and not to waste coal-oil keepin' the parlour lamp burning for me. And she got suspicious right away. Even when I told her who I was riding out with. You."

The gunsmith lowered his head. "She said a married man like me had no business ridin' out at night with a single feller like you. She said she wasn't no one's fool; she knew how single bucks went sneakin' out of town at night and went ridin' over to the homesteader places for some hired fun and all."

Thad, who did not know the gunsmith's wife very well, looked at his companion with a smoky gaze. "And what did you tell her?"

Al flung his arms wide. "What *could* I tell her? You never told me anything so what in hell could I

tell her?" The thick arms fell back to Al's sides.
"You got any coffee in there?"

Thad turned back into the office. Trent's recitation
had an unavoidably chilling effect. But as Thad
returned to his desk after motioning the gunsmith on
over to the stove and the coffeepot, he decided that
the Widow Haines would not be like that. Never in
all her borned days would she be like that. And
besides, if a man had something like that waiting for
him at home, what could he possibly be thinking of to
go riding up to the homesteader shanties? He sat
down, leaned back, sighed loudly and missed seeing
the peculiar stare he got from Al Trent. Not just
because the coffeepot was cold, but also because it
was empty.

The balance of the day passed slowly. Trent
returned to his shop after visiting the liverybarn to
make certain his private saddle animal was fully fed
and generously grained. Thad Mercer went down
there also, a little later, for the same purpose, and
encountered John Billings who was just leaving his
horse before going on over to the bank, first, then on
down to the mail-corner of the general store,
secondly, and finally, to the cafe for supper and the
saloon for poker and whisky.

Thad said, "Just met some folks who bought Red
Rock ranch. A brother and sister. They're up at the
boarding-house. Name of Haines."

Old Billings put a shrewd long stare upon the
lawman before saying, "Hell; I been running cattle
over there since old Reg passed on. Now maybe I'll
have to move them off."

Thad agreed. "I'd guess you'd have to move them,

but those folks didn't say whether they had cattle or not, but they figure to move onto the place so I'd figure they expect to get some cattle and run them out there."

"Good grassland," muttered Billings, then he brightened slightly as he said, "Maybe they're just greenhorns; after a year or two out here maybe they'll go back where they come from like most of them do. Tell you what I'll do—just leave the cattle over there until they try to make me move them."

Thad faced the older man slowly. "Get your gawddamned cattle off their Red Rock range," he said with such sudden fierceness old Billings was taken aback. "If you want to work something out with them, go talk to them, but it's their range and you've never had any right on it!"

Thad turned and walked briskly away. Old Billings stood rooted, and after a moment he said aloud, "I'll be double-damned if that's not one of the most unpredictable human beings I ever run across."

The liveryman, hearing a voice, came over and said, "What did you say, Mister Billings?"

Old John turned on him like a catamount. "Gawddammit can't a man ever have a little conversation with himself around here that you don't have to come along and get nosy!"

He stamped irately up out of the barn's shadowy long runway leaving the liveryman to stand where old John had formerly stood, looking just as bewildered and baffled.

11

LOST AND FOUND!

Not everybody was good to make a long horseback ride with, but Al Trent was, probably because after they had left town and were loping easily across the dusky range, he asked no questions and seemed entirely content to just be riding out.

Maybe he was. As he'd said earlier, he did not get a chance to leave the shop often.

On top of that it was a bland autumn night. In this part of the country it would remain bland almost every night right on up until Christmastime, and sometimes for a month beyond. There were a lot of rangemen who chose this area to winter in just for that reason—not exclusively because the nights were bland but also because the days were usually golden and warm and peaceful, too.

Al did not smoke, so when the lawman twisted up his first cigarette of the evening and pointed onward towards the foothills, the gunsmith tartly said, "If we're manhuntin' tonight, Marshal, and you go ridin' up through the dark suckin' on one of those filthy cigarettes, you might just as well play a harmonica."

Thad lowered his arm, changed what he had been about to say, and instead made a caustic comment.

"And you were telling me how cranky womenfolk are!"

They were mid-way to the foothills with the town lost to sight down the rearward late evening before Thad finally explained what he had in mind. When he finished explaining about George Beaudry, finished explaining what old Jase Beal had told him, and summed it up, he put it succinctly.

"If it's him and I sure got a powerful hunch that it is—then I'm gambling that when he thought of a place to camp in the Almarjal territory, he thought of *Aqua Frio* spring."

That seemed to fit well enough with Al's speculations, but the gunsmith had something more on his mind. "*Three* of them? Why didn't we fetch along a couple more fellers—or maybe a full posse?"

"Because two fellers won't make as much noise nor run as much risk of getting found out. That's why. And we're not going to brace them, we're just going to find out if they're up here ... You sure you can find the place in the dark?"

Trent rolled up his eyes. "Would I be out here riding around where there might be three armed renegades, if I didn't figure I could hide if I had to? Of course I can find the place in the dark. I been up there a hundred times during hunting season. One time I even spooked three In'ians who was campin' there on a pothunt of their own."

Thad absently nodded his head, then said, "That darned old John Billings was going to keep right on running his damned cattle on the Red Rock range even after he knew the Haineses had bought it?"

"The who had bought it?"

"Haines. Those folks I pointed out to you this afternoon as they headed for the rooming-house."

"You didn't tell me their names."

"I didn't?"

"No. Well, I don't think you did ... And what's this got to do with what we're doin' out here? Tell me something. These three outlaws—are they notorious and all?"

"No dodgers on them that I could find," replied Thad, swinging back to their earlier discussion. "My guess is that they're rangemen who've decided this is an easier way to make a living than cowboying."

"Almost anything is easier," muttered burly Al Trent as he stood in the stirrups in an effort to see onward where the up-coming foothills should be. "I'm no gunfighter, so I hope if we got to fight those fellers—."

"We're not going to fight them," exclaimed the lawman, "unless you blunder around and land us smack-dab in the centre of their camp." He too stood in his stirrups. "Where do we leave the horses and continue on foot?"

Al sank down again. "Walk ... damn it?"

"You want to ride up where our horses scent their horses and nicker?"

Trent let go a rattling big sigh. "You're not a very pleasant feller for a man to ride out with. All right; we'll go maybe another mile, leave the horses just inside the up-ended foothill country and climb the mountains on foot to where there's a slot atop a forested ridge where we'll be able to look right down at the springs. Damn; if you'd told me there was all this hikin' to do I'd have wore my shoes instead of these blasted cowhide boots which weigh a ton."

They found a spot to tether the horses. Al knew this country even better than he had said he did. When they walked away carrying carbines and leaving spurs looped around saddlehorns back yonder, he passed along through the deceptive early nightfall poor light and landed them squarely upon a good game-trail. They kept to this for three-quarters of an hour then Al turned off to their right, which was easterly, and hiked across a fairly flat ridge where the pines were thick until they encountered a gravel ledge. From that point on the trees were more sparse and nowhere nearly as robust as they had been elsewhere.

It was dark. In among the forest monarchs it was like walking inside a boot. Al never wavered and never paused. He ploughed right along, turning his head now and then to glance back as though he did not expect Thad to be there.

Eventually, when Trent halted and grounded his Winchester he said, "Dead ahead a few hundred yards and we'll be at the slot. From there you can look northward, and down below'll be the open little glen where the spring is. By now they'd ought to have their supper fire going."

But there was no supper fire. When they eventually halted in full darkness, not even having to bother about being discreet and stand near some of the sickly pines, they could make out the pale glade down below and dead ahead, but it was just as dark as all the rest of the broken country round about.

Al Trent frowned. "You sure this is where your outlaws camp?"

Of course Thad was not sure. He leaned down on his grounded Winchester studying the onward hush and gloom. If they had already cooked supper there would still be a lingering scent of it, and there was none. Also, it was unlikely that this far back, this safe from accidental discovery, those outlaws would not have kept their fire burning.

"I'm beginning to get a bad feeling," he muttered, and lifted the Winchester to the crook of his arm as he said, "Come along. We've come this far, might as well go whole-hog."

From here on the gunsmith let Thad lead the way. Starlight was not bright enough yet, and there was no moon at all. There might not be any moon tonight, Thad did not recall whether there was supposed to be one or not, and as he made his careful way down the north slope of their ridge he did not think about moonlight.

If he had guessed wrong about this being their campsite, then he could just as easily have guessed wrong about other things as well.

All he needed now was to have to explain to old John Billings among others, that he had been wrong, that what he had felt so confident about was pure hogwash all the way.

The gunsmith leaned and touched Thad's shoulder, then raised a hand to his lips for silence. Onward somewhere, not too distant even though it was very soft when they heard it, was a sound of some large animal moving either drowsily or heavily down from up above the spring-glade.

Thad said, "Bear. Just great; just what we needed to run into when we're on foot!"

They remained where they were until that sound, which did not seem to come closer although it kept shuffling back and forth, finally stopped altogether. If it were indeed a prowling bear, perhaps one which had recently filled up from a bee-tree and now sought cold water, not only to drink but also to bathe his smarting face in, he must have detected man-scent otherwise he would have kept right on coming.

After five minutes of listening and waiting, Al tapped Thad again and gestured onward with his Winchester.

They did not have far to go to enter the small glen. It was roughly three acres in size, had no trees closer to the spring than that, and had ripgut grass nearly stirrup-high throughout its small area.

Thad halted, looked up where they had heard that 'bear' and finally made a disgusted pronouncement. "Damned horse!"

They went over there and looked more closely. The reason their 'bear' had not come closer was because he was tethered where he could graze a little but where he could not walk out of the trees on the north side of the glade. He was clearly thirsty, which was what had made him stir restlessly moments earlier. Al went over to untie him and take him back to the spring to drink. As Thad started back, the horse bogged his head a little and once or twice minced a little. The gunsmith stopped, hauled the horse around until he was facing in the direction where he had ducked his head, then Al said, "Hey; isn't that a couple of bedrolls yonder behind those trees?"

It was not a couple of bedrolls it was *three* bedrolls. Thad examined each one without disturbing them very much. He also found three sets of saddlebags suspended from a low pine limb back in there, and he took them down, looking carefully inside each pouch while the horse impatiently yanked at the rope until the gunsmith swore at him, but took him on down to the spring to fill up.

When Trent came back to re-tie the gratified big bay horse, Thad was leaning against a rough-barked old pine tree. "Sure as hell," he informed the gunsmith, "it's their camp. But where are they?"

Al turned away to finish caring for the horse as he casually said, "Out making a raid, most likely. They sure as hell didn't leave, not and leave their possibles here."

Thad turned to silently watch the gunsmith return the horse to his tree, tie him, and walk back. Without thinking, the gunsmith had probably hit the nail squarely on the head. If the outlaws were not in their camp at night, and they surely weren't down at the saloon in town where they'd risk being identified— then they sure as hell *were* out somewhere making another blasted raid.

The gunsmith looked around. There were clear indications that three men had been camping here off and on for quite some time. A couple of weeks, maybe, or even longer. Trent waited patiently until the lawman had done his thinking and was gazing off in the direction of the big bay horse, then Trent said, "We could set up an ambush throughout this area slick as a whistle. It being dark and all."

Thad did not argue, he simply said, "Come along,"

and without explaining further led the way back as they came to this spot. Al Trent did not really feel too bad about not having his suggestion adopted. As he had said before, he was not a gunfighter. What he could have authoritatively added was that while he was not fast with handguns, and was not even very accurate with them, he was an excellent rifle and carbine marksman thanks to long years of practice and professional interest.

By the time they got back atop their ridge and had to pause to catch their breath, the gunsmith had it figured out. "You want to catch them flat-footed with a posse. Take them alive, is that it?"

That was indeed it, but there was more to it than that. What Thad especially did *not* want was to be up here when the outlaws returned. He did not want them to have any idea at all that someone had figured out enough about them to be this close—and those tethered horses were back down where he and Al Trent had left them.

It was too much of a risk. If the outlaws came up-country through the foothills which he was certain they would do, the chances were great that whether they actually saw two tethered saddle horses or not, either their horses would pick up the scent and perhaps nicker, or the tethered horses would do that. In either case it could amount to something a lot worse than trying to ambush the three renegades. It could also amount to a bushwhack in reverse—then a speedy escape by those three fleeing outlaws.

He said nothing of any of this. In fact he made such a hurry out of their rush back to their animals that when they finally got there and the gunsmith, who was unaccustomed to this sort of exertion, leaned on his horse as he breathed hard and said, "Gawddammit, what's the rush?" Thad still did not explain until they were on horseback riding easterly towards the stage road in order not to be in the foothills at all, if those three wanted men came loping along.

By the time he had made his explanation the gunsmith did not even care. All he wanted to do was catch his breath.

It was after midnight when they got back to town. In fact as Al Trent had prophesied earlier, it was close to early morning when they left their tired horses with the baggy-eyed liverybarn nighthawk and paused out front in the cooling night before going their separate ways.

"Not a darned word," admonished Thad.

The burly gunsmith cocked a jaundiced eye. "I don't talk in my sleep, and after what I been through tonight I'm going to sleep until noon tomorrow."

"Tomorrow night we'll do it again," Thad said. "Take a band up there. Al, we've got to get a posse up there without being heard."

Trent was as confident of being able to accomplish this as he had been of being able to get them up there to the spring this night.

"I'll be ready come sundown," he exclaimed. "I know we can do it. There is just one thing."

"Such as?"

"What darned big lie can I tell my wife two nights in a row?"

Thad turned away. "You're an ingenious feller.

You told me so when you were warning me against all womenfolk. You'll think of something."

Their bootsteps made hollow echoes as they left the vicinity of the liverybarn. They were the only two people abroad, and after Al Trent turned off to head eastward towards his modest cottage, that left only the town constable walking up Main Street.

He crossed over just south of the jailhouse, stepped up over in front of the general store and started past in the direction of the darkened saloon, then halted to see if he had indeed heard something or if it had been his imagination.

The sound came again, a light and muffled but very insistent tapping noise. He walked back towards the general store, reached to try the door, found it unlocked, drew his Colt and stepped inside without making a sound.

But there was no act of burglary in progress, it had already been committed. Walt Winters was lying behind his dry-goods counter within sight of his torn-loose cash drawer, tied hand and foot, and gagged.

Thad put up the gun, stepped back there and wordlessly knelt to free Winters. The storekeeper sputtered behind his gag and rolled his eyes. "Just shut up and be still," stated Constable Mercer as he dug out his pocket-knife and went to work cutting Walt's bonds.

12

MERCER MAKES PLANS

They went back to Walt's little cluttered office where there was a bottle, and as Walt lighted the lamp and went in search of two glasses he explained how it had happened.

"I sometimes work late. You can't get clerks nowadays who'll lift a finger after five o'clock ... Here it is; I knew I'd hid it somewhere ..." He brought forth the bottle and two glasses, set them upon his desk and poured.

"Somebody came along and rattled the roadway door. At first I wasn't going to pay any attention, but he rattled hell out of it and I figured maybe it was Doc or someone else with some sort of emergency." He offered Thad a full glass of whisky, did not wait to see if the lawman drank it, but tipped back his head and flung his own straight jolt down, then shuddered, set aside the glass and said, "Three of them. I figured it was just one man, but there was three of them. One at the door and the minute I opened up the other pair walked in, but one feller stayed back out by the door, sort of a look-out I expect. The other pair took me down here to the office, and after I'd opened the safe and showed them it was empty of everything except my books and some bills and manifests, they took me back to the cash-drawer and didn't even let me unlock it; one feller picked up a prise-bar and busted it."

Thad said, "How much did they get?" and that seemed to set the storekeeper off all over again. "How much? Gawddammit, Thad, almost every night since you been around here you made a round after supper, rattling doors and all. Tonight—the one damned night—"

Mercer was a little tired, and more than just a little irritable, so he said, "I asked how much they got. If you want to make a complaint about me not being able to be in two places at the same time, go to the next Town Council meeting. How - much - did - they - get!"

Winters sat at the desk and reached to refill his sticky little glass as he answered. "A damned thousand dollars."

The silence dragged out until Walt finished filling his glass and turned, gazing upwards. "Well. ...?"

"You had one thousand dollars in cash in that wooden drawer, Walt?"

Winters offered the bottle. Mercer declined with a single head-shake so the storekeeper put the bottle aside and did not look up again. "I got a load of freight coming first thing in the morning," he muttered. "I pay on the barrel-head. If you're in my business and you don't do that, freighters dilly-dally all over the territory before they bring your freight on in."

Thad was sceptical. "A thousand dollars in freight?"

"Well, not exactly ... There were some greenhorns came over this afternoon and established credit with me so's when they get set up they can send in a hired hand—if they find one—to fetch back—."

"Wait a minute. What strangers? Their name wouldn't be Haines would it?"

Winters nodded and picked up the whisky glass. "Yeah. A feller named Norman Haines and his sister—who is also named Haines." Walt sat holding the glass aloft as he turned and looked at the lawman. "She's a widow, but her name's the same as his—that's strange, isn't it? So I asked; she married a feller named Haines who wasn't any relation at all. I'll bet that don't happen very often."

Thad settled against the wall and went to work making a smoke. After lighting up and deciding that the whisky was beginning to get to Walt Winters, he said, "How much of that money belonged to those people?"

"Half."

Thad shook his head at the storekeeper. "Why the damned cash-drawer, Walt, instead of the safe?"

Winters stiffened a little at the constable's tone. "It wouldn't have made a darned bit of difference. Two cocked guns ten inches from my heart, and when they told me to open the safe by grabs I opened it. Cash-drawer or safe ..." Walt shrugged and leaned back in his old swivel chair.

"The one who stayed out by the door. ..."

"That's the one I didn't see too good, but the other two were cowboys. They needed to shave and they were shaggy-headed like sure-enough desperadoes."

Thad trickled smoke. "One was six feet or a shade

better, grey-eyed, had sandy hair and didn't act like he knew a lot about being an outlaw. The other feller was a little shorter, had blue eyes, and grinned or smiled a lot. All three of them had shaggy beards and they—."

"For Chris' sake if you know who they are, Marshal, how's come you don't have them locked in the jailhouse?" demanded the storekeeper, making an effort to keep the slur out of his voice.

Thad let that go past. "The man at the door was shorter, thicker, and dark."

"I told you I didn't ... Yeah, the build is right. He wasn't as tall as the other pair."

Thad stepped to the cuspidor at desk-side and sank his cigarette butt, then turned and said, "Do you remember a family named Beaudry who used to live here in town—well—on the north-easterly outskirts of town?"

Winters did not even hesitate. "Of course I knew them. The folks died and the kids flew the coop. I met a pedlar in town last summer who said he'd met a lady out in San Francisco who was from here, and now she's running a restaurant out there with her husband. Her name was Beaudry. She'd be the daughter."

"The man at the front door, Walt, the one who made a point of not letting you see his face, or seen him up close—was the general build right for George Beaudry, the lad of that family?"

Winters had to hedge. "Over the years ... It's been quite a spell, Marshal. Even when they was around here I didn't get to know the youngsters very well—and I never wanted to know the father very well because he was darned poor pay." Winters pursed his lips and stared. "That's who one of them was—young Beaudry?"

Thad ignored that to say, "What are you going to tell those greenhorns, Walt, about their missing five hundred dollars? They been in town one damned day, and get cleaned out."

Winters reacted with indignation. "It's not my fault. If folks got to place the blame ..." He saw the look on Mercer's face and did not finish it. Then he arose and flapped his arms. "What the hell is the country coming to? Robbed right here in my own store, right on the main road of town!"

"Next time walk a hundred yards up to the bank," said Thad, and hid a yawn as he turned towards the office door.

"Just overnight," exclaimed Walter Winters. "I been in business here a lot of years and never before had anything like this happen. Just overnight was all I figured to keep the money here."

Thad said, "Yeah. I'll see you tomorrow. Good night."

Winters squawked. "Wait a minute. I got a right to know what you figure to do—if you know who those men are." He trailed the constable to the front doorway and beyond, to the darkened roadway.

Thad said, "I aim to go to bed, that's what I aim to do. Good night!"

Winters remained in the doorway. All around him Almarjal was hushed and dark and layered over with a great depth of pre-dawn stillness.

By the time Thad got to his room up at the

boarding-house his irritability had atrophied but his resolve had become more bleak than ever.

The gunsmith's casual remark back up yonder in the mountains had been accurate right down to the last syllable. The reason no one had been at the outlaw-camp was indeed because the three renegades had been out on another raid, and this time the man who had not done too well with the stagecoach had clearly done a lot better at the general store—while George Beaudry discreetly prevented the storekeeper from possibly recognising him, and while the other rangerider had looked on.

Just before closing his eyes for what remained of the night Thad decided that in the morning he would ride out to JB. If he were going back up there to the cold water spring with a posse, he was not going to take any townsmen unless he had to—with the exception of Al Trent.

For this kind of thing he felt rangemen would be better.

He did not think of the brother and sister team again until after breakfast the following morning when he made a point of getting to the cafe early in order to be able to avoid all the furore and arti-culation news of the midnight-robbery would cause.

He probably would not have thought of them then, either, except that when he crossed the road to his office, Norman Haines was just leaving the general store, with Walter Winters trailing a trifle diffidently after him. Haines saw Thad Mercer and veered over towards the jailhouse.

Thad held the door for him without a greeting or a smile. For some confounded reason every time

something illegal happened, lately, folks blamed
Marshal Mercer, and hell's bells he was the one
person they should *not* blame.

Haines was still attired in his peg-top pants and his
little curly-brim hat when he said, "I had to get a
letter off aboard the dawn stagecoach, Marshal.
Otherwise I'd have slept a little longer." He studied
Thad. "You know about the robbery, of course."

"I know about it, Mister Haines, and I'm sorry as
hell about your loss."

"Thank you," stated the bronzed, wide-shouldered
man. "The storekeeper said you know who the
outlaws are?"

"Not exactly *know* them, Mister Haines. I've yet
to lay eyes on any of them—but I have a fair idea
about them."

"And. ...?"

Thad motioned towards a chair as he went over to
perch upon the edge of his desk. "I'm going to do
what I can, Mister Haines," he averred. "With some
luck we may even get your money back. But that's
just a wild guess."

Thad smiled. "Hell of a way for a town to
welcome greenhorns, isn't it?"

Instead of answering the question Haines said,
"Marshal, if you need a volunteer for posse-
riding. ..."

Thad looked at the button shoes and peg-top pants
and that elegant little curly-brimmed hat. "I think
I'll have enough men when the time comes," he
replied, "but thanks anyway."

"All the same, since it was my money they made
off with, I'd like a chance to go after them with you.

Otherwise I suppose I'll have to hire someone to help me scout over the countryside. Marshal, I have no intention of staying in town when someone with my money in his pocket is riding off."

Thad had no aversion to taking Norman Haines along. It was simply that he had some pre-arrived-at opinion of Haines as a town-man who had probably never done much horsebacking let alone much—if any—manhunting. On the other hand, Thad would just as soon not have Haines traipsing over the countryside, just in case ....

"You can ride with the posse when I get it organised," Thad told the other man. "I'll look you up when we're ready."

He did not say how long it might be before the possemen rode out, nor did he explain that they would not actually be going out on a manhunt since he already knew where the renegades had their camp. All he said in addition to the rest of it, as he escorted Haines out into the brightening new-day morning, was that he hoped Haines—and his sister-in-law or whatever she was to Mr Haines—did not form their first impression of the countryside from this interlude.

The handsome man turned and smiled. "We're not children, Marshal, we understand, and incidentally she is my *sister*, not my sister-in-*law*. The names are the same for a simple reason. Her husband was also named Haines. A coincidence, wouldn't you say? But not all that much of a coincidence."

Thad smiled and watched Norman Haines head over towards the cafe for breakfast. As he turned to re-enter the office, Blaine Harper came bustling over from the opposite side of the roadway and Thad sighed, left the door open, went back to his desk and waited.

But Harper did not arrive that soon. Someone out in the roadway buttonholed him. Thad could hear them talking, could distinguish the impatience in the banker's voice as he attempted to get clear. Thad smiled to himself.

Later, when the banker finally walked in he acted irritable. Thad did not allow him any opportunity to start another argument. The last time they had talked in here, Thad had almost lost his temper.

"If folks don't make use of the bank, even for overnight," Thad said while smiling at the banker, "why then I expect they got to take their chances."

"Exactly," exclaimed the banker, his expression brightening slightly. "Exactly, Marshal. That's what banks are for—to cache your money in so's you won't have to leave it in a wooden cash-drawer to be stolen by the first outlaw who walks in. I wish there was some way to make a town ordinance of that."

"I'll bet you do," murmured Thad Mercer, and went over to push kindling into the little iron stove so he could make a pot of coffee. "What can I do for you, Mister Harper?"

"I wanted to say John Billings says you are doing exactly right."

Thad went right on working over at the stove. What John Billings thought did not mean that much to him, not even when it was favourable.

"And of course I agree with that one hundred per cent," stated Harper.

Thad with his back still to the banker, smiled at the front of the little iron wood-stove, and winked.

"And we—all the fellers who got a financial interest in the bank, you see—we all talked it out and are willing to offer a two hundred dollar reward for the apprehension of that son of a bitch who robbed the bank."

Thad set the pot atop a burner and turned back towards his desk. "I'll make a note of that, Mister Harper ... Two hundred dollars for the bank-robber." He looked up. "Dead or alive?"

"I reckon that's how it's usually done, isn't it?"

"Yeah."

"Then make it two hundred dead or alive. And Marshal, I have a feeling Walter Winters is thinking of adding another hundred to that."

Thad tossed aside his pencil. "I'll talk to him about it, Mister Harper. Anything else?"

"Well—no, not exactly. I was just wondering—do you have any ideas about that bank-robber?"

"That's about all I do have, Mister Harper: Ideas. But things may look up. I hope so. And if they do I'll make a point of seeing that you are told." Thad fixedly smiled. "Thanks for coming by."

After getting rid of the banker Thad blew out a big breath, reached for his hat and started out the door on his way down to the liverybarn to get his horse and head for JB.

John Billings was leaning on the tie-rack directly in front of him, tethering a *grulla* horse which was still in the big rawhide breaking hackamore. Billings looked up, grunted, finished with the horse and stamped on around heading into the office.

13

ANOTHER DAY

Thad Mercer was a little like Al Trent even though Thad got much more of an opportunity to ride out, so the fact that John Billings had arrived in town this early saved Thad the long ride out to JB, but on the other hand he was mildly regretful because he liked that ride.

Especially today, he preferred not to be in town all day. He had no intention of making any public announcement of his plans, and if he remained in town that same disapproval was certainly going to be resurrected after Walt Winters had also been robbed.

But at least as long as John Billings was in the office he would be unable to go anywhere. The big old cowman eyed the stove but said nothing despite the enticing aroma of boiled coffee over there, and after his lifelong custom Billings got settled in a chair, allowed plenty of time to pass first, then eventually spoke. Thad assumed those privileges went along with being one of the largest and most success-ful cowmen in the countryside.

"We're missing some horses," he ultimately announced. "But there's no way of telling when they was stolen because they was out with the loose-stock on the north-westerly horse-range. Only discovered it yesterday when the rangeboss sent a couple of the riders out to fetch in fresh usin' animals. Four head. One in particular I hate to lose. Big bay horse, got the best rein on him you'll see in this country."

Thad sighed, thinking back to the big bay horse up at *Aqua Frio* spring. "Sixteen hands," he murmured. "Fairly young, hackamore-horse, Mister Billings?"

The older man sat and glowered. After a while he nodded his head when he said, "You know about him too, do you?"

Thad smiled. "I know about *a* tall, nice-looking leggy bay horse."

"Got JB on his left shoulder, Marshal?"

Neither Thad nor Al Trent had paid that much attention to the horse last night. "Didn't look, Mister Billings, but I was going to ride out to the ranch this morning and ask if I could borrow three, four of your riders, and if you cared to go along too, I'd show you the big bay horse."

"Those bastards got him, have they?"

Thad required no better description, and before answering it he said, "I got a fair notion where they are camped. Riders can't just head up there in broad daylight or they'd be seen for five miles before they even got close. So, I had in mind leaving about sunset this evening."

Billings did not even hesitate. "Where do I meet you with my crew—and there should be more than just that one horse. How about the others?"

Thad had only seen one big bay. He was not certain this was the stolen bay, but he felt reasonably confident it was. As for another three head—he had no difficulty imagining where they might be—under Beaudry and his renegade partners—but you couldn't hang horsethieves by just guesswork, so he said, "If the other three horses are up there, with a little luck we might get a crack at them too, tonight ... I'll leave town before sunset with a man named Haines, and also with Al Trent. We'll head due west and meet you out there somewhere. But we dassn't try for the foothills until dark."

Billings nodded. "All right ... This Haines feller—same one you got up onto your horse about when I mentioned having JB cattle on Red Rock range?"

Thad felt heat in his cheeks so he went to the stove as he said, "Same man." As he filled two tin cups he also said, "Walter Winters was robbed last night," and turned to hand Billings one of the cups. The cowman accepted the cup and continued to hold it at arm's length as he stared.

"The general store—raided?"

"Yeah. Same three or I'm nuttier than a pet 'coon."

"Riding my horses?"

Thad shrugged. "Time will tell."

"Where'n hell was you last night—how could three outlaws ride right up into town and—."

"I was in the mountains locating their camp, Mister Billings. And if you know any way for one lawman to be in two places at the—."

"Don't flare up at me, confound it, I was just trying to figure out what-all happened around here last night."

"I told you what happened. You can go across and talk to Walt for the rest of it."

They regarded one another, then John Billings slapped lean legs and stood up. He was a tall, gaunt old man. "You ride west at sundown—we'll be out there. One question: where'll we head from there?"

"Past the foothills on into the mountains. But don't tell anyone, even back at the ranch, or I'll lose a bank-robber and you'll be out four head of horses and twenty-five hundred dollars."

The old cowman departed, looking as bleak as he could look. He had an odd characteristic of becoming angry slowly and with an increasing venom for some time after whatever it was which had irritated him had happened. Blaine Harper had seen evidence of this not long before, and so had the liveryman. Now it was the turn of Walter Winters, and he was as unsuspecting as the others had been when he met old Billings just inside the doorway of his store and started complaining about the kind of law-enforcement and protection they had around Almarjal.

"Cleaned me out of a thousand dollars, by gawd, and I lay tied like a turkey until nearly sunup before Mercer came along!"

"Well, what in the hell was you doing, keeping that much money in your store overnight—or any other time?" growled Billings. "I never gave you much credit for brains and now I give you less ... Just fetch me the ranch mail and set your clerk to filling this list!"

Winters stood staring, then turned without another word to go after JB's mail. On the way he told his clerk to go get the old cowman's list. He also told him to be discreet because the old devil was in one of his vile moods.

But there were compensating factors. The old cowman's interludes of ire never seemed to last very long. In fact when the handsome woman in the superbly-fitting pearl grey outfit walked into the store and old Billings saw her, he forgot about being disagreeable altogether and when the clerk came diffidently to take his list, Billings beamed upon the man, handed over the list, then leaned to quietly ask who *that* was.

The clerk turned, stood a moment just admiring her, then turned back with a sad answer. "Never seen her before yestiddy in all my life, Mister Billings." He scuttled away with the list and Walt Winters returned with two worn-looking letters and an even worse-looking newspaper.

Billings asked Walt the same thing, and he at least could give a little information although he did not know Betsy Haines as well as he knew her brother.

Billings listened, watched the handsome woman, and when Walt finally grudgingly said, "That thousand dollars they stole off me last night—well—five hundred of it belonged to that lady and her brother."

Billings stared. "What in hell was you doing, Walter, competing with the bank? Since when have you got the facilities to protect folks's money in this fly-trap store of yours?"

Winters reddened. "Keep your voice down," he hissed. "It wasn't my idea. Her brother wanted to establish credit and put up that money to sort of show good faith."

"And you took it—you old fraud? What do you think we got a bank in Almarjal for? I felt sorry for you before. Now I'm glad they raided you!"

The cowman picked up his mail, stuffed it into a jacket pocket and went over where the handsome woman was standing before a glass case of genuine mother-of-pearl buttons and some of the latest style button-hooks—with real bone handles.

He took off his hat to reveal snow-white hair, smiled and introduced himself, and as the beautiful eyes came around to coolly make their assessment he mentioned the stolen money, and this time her gaze sharpened. So far, this early morning, no one had told her. She had been abed in a separate room at the boarding-house when her brother had got dressed and gone forth, and until right this minute she had no idea anything had happened, so now as her interest in the rugged old rancher quickened she asked details, and as he supplied her with them he got a bad feeling that he had jumped in and taken over someone else's job.

He looked around, but Walt Winters was busy with customers. Then he caught sight of Thad Mercer across the road from the corner of his eye and grasped at this straw by saying, "If you'd like, ma'am, I'll take you over and you can talk to Marshal Mercer."

She too turned and watched as two horsemen in the roadway saluted the lawman on their way past. They called something to him, grinning, and he sang out an answer, also grinning.

She said, "Mister Billings, is he the only lawman in this lawless place?"

Old John scratched his chin trying to decide which part of that question to answer first. Then he said, "This here is just about the most law-abiding town you've ever been in. And yes, Thad Mercer's the only—."

"Didn't you just tell me the place was raided last night—the general store *and us*? That doesn't sound awfully law-abiding to me, Mister Billings."

"Well, but before that we almost never had trouble." He thought of his own recent encounter, and of the even more recent robbery of the stagecoach, and fell to rubbing his jaw again. "Thing is—times are changing, Miss Haines. Folks are not quite as law-abiding as they were in my day."

"It is *Mrs* Haines, Mister Billings. As for times changing—it seems to me they've never stopped changing." She smiled at him. "It was kind of you to take an interest. My brother and I have never been this far into the west before. Incidentally, are those your JB cattle which are grazing over our Red Rock range?"

He saw that beautiful smile, and because he was an older individual he could see beyond the beauty to the layers of iron in Betsy Haines's character. "Marshal Mercer told me I'd ought to get them off your grass," he told her. "Of course, if you folks got no animals, and it being pretty late in the year and all for stockin' up, I figured I'd make you an offer for your feed for the balance of the year."

She seemed receptive and said she would tell her brother, who would then no doubt ride over and talk to old Billings. Then she turned to follow the lawman's course as he strode up in the direction of the gunsmith's shop, for a while she had no more to say.

Billings watched her face, picked up the object of her interest and began slowly putting a couple of small pieces of some kind of evidence side by side.

Finally, as the clerk came over to return his list and explain that the croacker-sack near the door had everything inside it which had been on the list, Billings nodded as the clerk walked away, caught the attention of the beautiful woman, then invited her to ride over to JB. He also invited her brother over, but her impression was that he had made that latter offer as a sort of afterthought; as a sort of tribute to the *mores* of the era when he had been taught his manners.

She accepted, smiled at him, and turned away.

Old John shuffled to the door, picked up the croacker-sack, turned once to gaze at her just one more time, then went on outside, and the first person he met was Sam Trotter from the bank. Sam was on his way up the road to work when he encountered John Billings, and because Sam was by nature a diffident man, and because old John Billings had a lot of money in the bank, Sam lifted a hand to his hatbrim as he said, "Good morning, sir."

Billings nodded. "Same to you. Sam; do you like to look at pretty women?"

Trotter's steps faltered, he stared disbelievingly at Billings. "Sir ...?"

"Pretty girls, damn it all; do you like to look at them?"

"Well; yes sir, I like to look at them," answered

Sam, casting sidelong glances close around. He did
not want anyone to hear this evil conversation.

John jutted his chin. "Amble inside the store. Go
ahead, damn it all. If you're a few minutes late at the
bank tell Blaine if he don't like it to go suck eggs.
Walk in there. She got a pearl grey dress on. Sam, if
you live to be as old as I am you'll never see another
one like that. Go look."

Trotter reached to run a finger under his celluloid
collar and gaze wistfully in the direction of the bank
where he longed to be. Sam was not a young man,
and before in his life had encountered dirty old men,
but never had he even imagined old John Billings
belonged to that category, and that made it all the
harder for him to believe it now.

"Go," commanded the old cowman. "Go inside the
store and look at her, confound it."

Sam Trotter obediently turned and walked into the
general store.

Billings shook his head and muttered to himself as
he shouldered the croacker-sack and struck out across
the road, where he'd left his horse tied at the
jailhouse hitchpole.

"Gawddamn young fellers nowadays just don't
have any gumption any more. My gawd, I never saw
a woman that all-round pretty in this lousy territory
in all the years I been out here. Never ... Mercer's a
blasted lucky young buck. If he don't overlook that
she's interested." Billings spat, stepped to his saddle
to lash the croacker-sack into place. "Or if he don't
get himself killed chasing after those lousy
renegades."

Max Jeeter the corralyard boss came along,

recognised Billings, and said, "You're in town right early this morning."

John ignored that to look around and say, "You want to see the prettiest woman you'll ever see in your life, Max?" He pointed. "Over yonder in the general store. Wearing a sort of pearly grey dress."

Jeeter did not say a word nor hesitate, he made a sharp and abrupt turn, stepped off the plankwalk and went in a bee-line towards the front entrance of the general store.

Billings nodded to himself and confided in his horse that maybe there was hope after all; not all the younger men in the territory were as measly as Sam Trotter was.

He swung aboard, turned his horse southward, rode to the lower end of town then booted the beast over into an easy little lope heading westerly. It was a warm, beautiful morning by this time. It was going to be a warm and magnificent day. What it would be like after nightfall was anyone's guess, but at least the *weather* promised to be bland.

14

THROUGH THE NIGHT

Constable Mercer led his pair of companions west from town just at dusk, and because the year was nearing its end there would be no lingering daylight, something he had taken into consideration before riding out. He preferred to reach the foothills as he had done the previous night, when visibility was extremely limited.

Haines and Al Trent got along very well, considering neither had spoken to the other until Thad had introduced them down at the liverybarn.

Norman Haines had made several changes today. One was in his attire, and regardless of how new everything looked, from the unscuffed cowhide boots to the sweat-free hat, the man inside looked 'Western' enough. He had looked that way to Thad when they had first met. Haines was wide-shouldered, lean and bronzed. He could pass anywhere as a rangerider.

Al Trent had acted slightly dubious at first, but by the time the trio was two-thirds of the way across JB range westerly, Trent and Haines were getting along as though they had been lifelong acquaintances.

To clinch it, they teamed up on Thad Mercer, and

this was something which Trent did with relish. Last night Thad had not been altogether amiable part of the time. Al had not forgotten. When they were far enough along to start thinking about encountering the JB men, Trent said, "Thad, if Old Man Billings rides along too, that's going to be a real trial for the rest of us."

Thad looked around. "A real trial?"

"Yeah. *Two* cranky fellers along."

Trent smiled broadly and Norman Haines grinned a little. He did not know Thad Mercer well enough to know whether he really was cranky or not, but he caught the implication at once.

Thad halted half a mile after that to listen. He heard them, finally, a fair distance onward and slightly to the north. Evidently Billings had been getting impatient and had started northward on his own. It was precisely because of this possibility that Thad had not told the cowman exactly where the renegade-camp was.

A horseman appeared dead ahead at a slow lope, hauled down, sat a moment studying the trio from town, then turned without a word to lead the way back.

Billings had his entire riding crew along except for the horse-wrangler, and he was a boy of sixteen. The rangeboss, the *cabalgador*—ranch horseman who did everything from shoe, to break, to doctor, to round up, ranch horseflesh—even the *cosinero*—ranch cook—and he was a man as old as John Billings who wore a perpetually vinegary expression.

Billings and his men were armed with handguns and saddleguns. The old cowman studied Al Trent, whom he knew, then switched to study the wide-shouldered man wearing the new hat, britches and boots. He knew who this was before being introduced. He probably would not have so gallantly nodded and brushed his hatbrim if he had not also known this man's sister.

Thad looked at the rangemen, most of whom he had come to know over the riding seasons because they came back to hire on each springtime. Even the ones he knew only by sight, though, left him satisfied about his posse. He lifted his reinhand.

"You ready?" he asked.

Without answering Billings turned northward.

It was a fair distance and as nightfall began to mantle the entire vast Almarjal plateau, he leaned to speak to the old cowman with whom he was riding stirrup up front.

"We'll let Al Trent take us in, and we'll leave the horses down below and walk most of the way."

Billings's reaction to that was similar to Trad's reaction last night. "Walk?" he said. "How far?"

"Mile and a half," replied Thad, sure he was minimising it but feeling justified on the grounds that he did not want to have an argument, nor to have to listen to old Billings groan and grumble.

It happened anyway. It might have happened if Thad had said only half a mile of walking.

"For twenty-five hunnert dollars I'll walk, Marshal, but by gawd nothing is going to make me like it ... By the way," the old man leaned like a conspirator. "I met Haines's sister ... You've met her?"

"Yes."

"Did you ever see a female-woman like that before in all your life?"

Thad shook his head. "No sir, I don't believe I have."

Billings continued to narrowly regard the lawman. He was upon the verge of saying more when Al Trent eased up on the lawman's far side to say he would lope ahead to make certain there was nothing close by, where they would leave their horses.

Thad was agreeable. "Take Haines with you."

After those two had gone ahead the JB riders bunched up closer around their leaders, Thad and old John Billings. Whatever it was the cowman had been thinking of a few moments past died right there. When Thad looked at him, Billings just hoisted wide, bony old shoulders, and let them fall. He did not open his mouth.

Not until Thad said, "I got to thinking this afternoon ... They've taken seventy-one hundred dollars, Mister Billings. That's one hell of a lot of money to come out of one place ... Maybe they won't be up there tonight. Maybe they are wise enough to figure they're not going to get much more, and that meanwhile the countryside will be stirred up."

"You mean—they won't be up there because they've rode on?"

Thad nodded. Old John Billings emitted a low groan, and whatever else he might have said about Betsy Haines was lost forever.

"It's just a guess," explained Mercer. "Just something I got to wondering about this afternoon."

Billings still said nothing. They rode for more than

half a mile before he opened his mouth again. "Then I'm going after them, with my crew. They can't have got much of a start, and I know this countryside better'n any man alive—they couldn't hide from me if they was In'ians."

Thad said, "Mister Billings, I didn't say they *had* pulled out. I just said *maybe* they had. I was thinking about all the money they have now. Most men would want to spend a little rather than just try to get some more."

"The hell with the money," growled old Billings. "I want those horses back, especially that long-legged big bay horse."

Thad considered the old man's craggy face for a moment wondering if *he* would ever get to the point in life where the welfare of four common everyday ranch using horses meant more than twenty-five hundred greenbacks.

They reached the foothills, turned slightly eastward at a quiet walk until they got around behind the low knoll where Al Trent and Norman Haines were waiting, and had to scatter out a little to find enough places to tie all those horses. Counting old Billings, the riders from JB totalled five men. Added to that were the trio from town. The result was a fairly formidable posse.

Trent would have led the way from here as he had previously done except that this time old Billings exerted his prerogative as chief of two-thirds of the posse. But he did not do it arbitrarily. He simply said, "Gents, I was huntin' and fishin' and explorin' up in here when you was—every blessed one of you was in three-cornered pants. And I been doing it up in here ever since. You just stay behind and be as quiet as mice, and I'll take you to the spring by a trail don't any of you know."

It was the truth; he knew an ancient Indian pathway which had not been used for so many years that except for the faintest of indentures up around the slopes, and these were all covered now by weedy-growth and layers of fallen leaves, it would have been difficult to discern the trail in daylight, let alone in the dark.

But it also happened to be a fairly lengthy procedure to employ this trail, because while it was clearly taking them higher as they followed it, it was also taking them east of the spring in such a manner that when they finally got around where they had the spring in sight, they were going to be northward, or completely around the spring and in behind it.

Why the old-time Indians had gone to all this bother instead of following along that gravelly ridge Trent and Mercer had utilised the previous night was anyone's guess at this very late date, but they would indeed have had a good reason—good to them at any rate—and it seemed to Thad Mercer that quite possibly the old-time neolithics had gone to all that bother because they had been by nature very cautious people.

He was right. Prehistoric redskins did not have whiteskins to face, the curse of their distant descendants, but they'd had even more deadly enemies among the wolfpacks and the lions and bears which had little to fear from fire-hardened little ash arrows.

They almost never made a direct approach to anything, not even their camps, but had arrived only after a very circuitous route which had allowed them to see their camp on all sides first, before they walked on in.

This was what old Billings had had in mind as he silently stalked ahead; they would be able to see the camp at the spring from more than just one point of vantage before they got close enough to set up their ambush.

It was an excellent idea, at least this particular night it was because there was a little fire burning at the camp. They picked up the smell of smoke long before the pathway allowed them to skirt around through trees on the east side of the little rip-gut meadow and actually eventually spy flames through the forest.

And horses. Billings halted with an upraised hand. He was holding his carbine in the upraised fist, for all the world like one of those gaunt old *anasazi* warriors who had formerly ruled this territory.

But the distance was too great for any of them to make a positive identification. All Thad was certain of was that there were seven saddle horses gorging out there on the rip-gut, which was the right number. If Beaudry's gang had stolen four JB horses, and already had three of their own. ...

JB's rangeboss was directly behind Thad and Al Trent. He leaned to whisper in a very dry tone. "If we don't catch 'em on the ground we're not goin' to catch 'em, gents."

Billings grunted and gestured. They struck out again. From this point now, their trail began to angle upwards and over on a different course, more to the east but on a long-spending curve which was going to take them around through the trees where that bay horse had been tethered the previous night, then on around still more until they were going southward again but over upon the west side of the camp.

Thad halted the posse eventually, having made up his mind to start organising their ambush. He detailed men to remain on the trail at intervals. By the time he and Billings were up where that bay horse had been—and no longer was, incidentally— they had strung men out on both sides, and nor- thward. Al Trent and Norman Haines had been left north of the camp. Al knew the trees up there from having looked after the horse in that vicinity the previous night.

Where Thad finally halted for the last man to be detached and positioned, old Billings leaned down and pointed. It was possible to see more than just the campfire now, through the trees, it was also possible to see mounded horse equipment, and at least one man who was sprawling with his back to an up-ended saddle as he smoked and gazed into the fire. The other two men were not yet visible.

Thad and Billings went onward, halted when they were in a part of the trail which came closer to the opening, and without a word passing between them, leaned upon their carbines and peered dead ahead where a short, stocky, dark man was rummaging through a scuffed pair of those big-pocketed army saddlebags some rangemen—not very many—pre- ferred. John Billings let his breath out slowly.

"That's the son of a bitch," he whispered. He did not explain anything, nor did he have to. Thad already had a description of the man who had raided the JB outfit. The only thing he had to do now was fit that description, that man over there, to a name, and that was not hard to accomplish.

If old Jase Beal had been along he could have made a positive identification. But Jase wasn't with them, and if he had been he could not have been any more convincing right now than Thad's intuition was.

"Beaudry," he muttered to John Billings. "George Beaudry."

A second man, lanky and lean, who could have been a few years older, strolled over to Beaudry and said something the hidden watchers could not distinguish. Beaudry answered in a tone of clear exasperation, but without raising his voice so they could not hear what he had said either. Then the third man came walking out there from where he had been sitting at the fire. He yawned, said, "Plenty of time to get ready in the morning," and yawned a second time.

Mercer and Billings heard that plainly enough. They also heard the other tall man answer it.

"If we can get about half organised before sunup that'd ought to give us enough of a start to be westerly through the damned hills before most folks is stirring. Won't even have no accidental meetings then."

The man who had yawned grinned crookedly. "You two are a regular pair of foxes, always tryin' to think ahead, then to think ahead of *that*."

"And you're alive because of it," stated Beaudry, but none of those men were yeasty or hostile, they were just blunt rangemen.

The protester was derisive when he said, "Alive

because of it? Hey George, they never so much as raised a gun at us—none of them. This has been like knockin' frogs off the bank into the creek with a long stick."

The other two men, Beaudry and Zack Harmon, exchanged a look and exaggeratedly wagged their heads to indicate how naive their partner was. They then went on getting their horse-gear organised.

Thad felt gratified. Clearly, those men over at their pleasant little camp had intended to pull out in the morning. One more day and there would have been a hell of a fine chance that the law—and the JB cowmen—never would have caught up in time to salvage any of that stolen money, or those four stolen saddle animals.

Billings leaned and brushed Thad's arm with his Winchester barrel. "Well? We going to stand out here all night—or what?"

There were two ways to accomplish what now had to be done. One way was to stroll out there and in a very low-key manner explain to the Beaudry gang that they were surrounded by armed and willing possemen. The other way was not to leave the protection of the trees, and to yell out to those men at the fire.

Thad did not know any of those men well enough to even make a half-accurate guess about how they would react, but he knew for a fact that if he strolled over there, even after announcing himself in advance, it was entirely possible someone might shoot him.

He pointed to a nearby big old stiff-limbed bull-pine for John Billings. He then stepped behind a nearby pine tree of his own.

15

THE MOUNTAIN MEADOW MEETING

The light was not the best, of course, and even at their campfire it was not as good as those hiding possemen could have wanted. Still, as Marshal Mercer watched those three outlaws where they were standing among the horse-equipment, he had an excellent view.

They were beginning to turn away from the saddlery when Thad called over to them without raising his voice very much.

"Beaudry! You three fellers stand still! This is a posse from Almarjal and you're surrounded!"

For two or three seconds it seemed as though the outlaws were not going to move. Clearly, they had been taken completely by surprise. Then the tallest of them, Zack Harmon, hurled himself back towards that mound of horse-gear clawing for his Colt as he dropped. Beaudry and the remaining man both moved a second later, striking the ground and trying to frantically roll into deeper grass.

Old Billings let off a profane squawk and fired. That was the first gunshot and it caught the man beside Beaudry flush. He arched his back up off the ground as tense as a steel spring, threw up his face and for a moment both Billings and Mercer saw his features, which were smoothed out with total astonishment. Then the man collapsed on his face and never moved again.

He was the man called Matt Hendry, the grinning cowboy who had robbed the bank in Almarjal. But right at this moment all the onlookers could be sure of was that, whoever he was, this uplands glade was as far as he was going, in *this* life anyway.

Beaudry and the man behind the saddlery opened up in Billings's direction, driving the irate old cowman back behind his bull-pine.

Thad had an idea that the possemen over across the camp in among the trees could see the exposed backs of those two outlaws. He would prefer taking them alive so he allowed the gun-racket to diminish then he sang out again.

"Beaudry, you damned fool! I told you—there are possemen on all sides of you—and in back where they can nail you! Leave it be! Quit trying to make a fight of it or you're going to end up dead like your friend!"

Again, for a moment or two it seemed that the surviving outlaws might take Mercer's advice. Then they both fired, and this time from different positions as they continued to back-crawl in their desperate attempt to get into the taller grass.

Over across the little meadow a man hooted, making a derisive Indian war-call. Then he fired and George Beaudry threshed wildly in the grass. The posseman made that same call and fired again. This time there was no response, so Thad Mercer guessed that Beaudry had been hit and killed, or had been shot unconscious and was out of it either way—or—

he had had a near thing and was lying hidden in the grass now waiting for his heart to stop thumping.

Billings knew who had made that war-cry and called over there. "Jeremy; can you see the bastards?"

Instead of an answer he got back the same cry again, and two ground-sluicing gunshots fired so fast they almost seemed to be the same gunshot.

This time a man in the grass twisted and fired back, and once more, for the last time, that hooting man let go his chilling war-cry.

A rattle of loose gunfire from three directions broke the momentary silence. From the north it was Trent and Haines, from the far side it was part of JB's riding crew—one of them over yonder was the man who had given the war-cry. From over on the east side where Mercer and Billings were, but a little farther northward, more JB rangemen cut loose.

Mercer lowered his gunhand and waited for a reaction out in the grass, and when there was none he called out there for the third time.

"Beaudry? You hear me? This is Constable Mercer from town. If you thought I was bluffing before, now you know better ... You fellers got no protection. We don't even have to see you, all we got to do is ground-sluice through the grass from all directions. Make up your mind what you want to do."

The silence dragged on. Thad heard old Billings moving stealthily from his place of concealment nearby and would have growled except that those men in the yonder grass would hear him, would probably surmise what Billings was trying to do— stalk them—and nail him.

Then a man spoke from somewhere out in the clearing, his voice pitched a little higher than normal and strained-sounding.

"All right. I ain't going to die in this lousy place if I don't have to. All right, Constable."

From the opposite side a man said, "Hey, lawman—I can see the son of a bitch! He's crawlin' north where them horses run to. Want me to nail him?"

Before Thad could speak the outlaw cried out loudly. "I told you, Constable—I quit. All right, I give up!"

Old Billings answered his rangeman across the meadow in a low, almost sullen-sounding tone of voice. "Naw, don't shoot the son of a bitch, Jeremy. Wait until we see what he's up to—*then* maybe we can shoot him!"

Thad exerted his authority at this point. He was not at all confident those JB rangemen would not kill that outlaw. In a sharp tone he said, "You fellers over yonder—watch him and that's all. You understand? Just watch him!" He paused, then addressed the fugitive again. "You out yonder in the grass—stand up without your weapons."

"Like hell," exclaimed the outlaw. "You heard those fellers; they'll shoot!"

"If they do," said Thad Mercer, "I'll shoot back. Now shut up and get up over there where I can see you!"

The outlaw arose very reluctantly. He did not face forward in Thad's direction, he was twisting to watch over his shoulder.

John Billings swore in the same sullen-sounding

tone and leaned to ground his Winchester and peer over where the outlaw was raising both arms overhead. "If that's Beaudry, I want him for horse-stealin' and armed robbery."

Thad ignored the cowman, walked around from behind his tree, gun still up and cocked. He knew that was not George Beaudry by the height alone, so he called out.

"Where are the others who were with you a few minutes back?"

"You hit Hendry. That first shot nailed Matt Hendry," the outlaw replied, then turned left and right looking around through the tall grass. "I don't know what happened to George."

Billings was beside himself. He yelled for the possemen to close in, to tighten the surround and not to allow Beaudry to escape.

If the men obeyed Thad saw no sign of it, but they could have been obeying, and as dark as it was out where most of them were, unless they made a lot of noise Thad would have got no indication.

"Stay where you are," he called annoyedly, then turned on Billings. "That goes for you too. And shut up!" He then faced their captive with an order. "Walk over towards the sound of my voice. Start walking!"

The outlaw did, he came on steadily for about thirty or forty feet, then recoiled and looked down as though he might have encountered a rattlesnake in the tall grass.

"Here's George Beaudry," he called out, and remained a moment longer to stare at something in the grass before responding to Thad's order to keep on walking.

From the north Al Trent and Norman Haines started walking southward separated by a distance of about fifty or sixty feet, each with his cocked Colt thrust forward as they approached the place in the grass where the captive had halted.

Thad felt like swearing, instead he did as all the other possemen were doing, he watched intently.

There was some consolation in the obvious fact that if Beaudry rose up from the grass to shoot, he would be unable to aim at but one of those stalking possemen, and while he was doing that the other one would have his chance for a shot at close quarters.

It did not work out that way. By the time the prisoner was close enough for Thad to growl at him to halt, Haines and Trent were standing out there, one on each side of the place where the captive had located Beaudry. The gunsmith leaned, looked intently, then straightened back and said, "Thad? He's either dead or bad hit, but either way he's just lyin' here."

Other possemen came forth, finally. The fight was finished, the pursuit and capture had been completed.

Old Billings stalked over and glowered at the captive. "What's your name?" he snarled, and the outlaw answered very promptly. "Zachary Harmon!"

"Which one are you," snarled Billings, thrusting his hawkish face closer. "The bank-robber?"

"No sir."

"You ain't Beaudry, the feller who raided me at the ranch, so then you'll be the feller who raided the general store last night, and the southbound stagecoach before that."

"Yes sir, I stopped the stage and helped raid the store last night."

"We'd ought to hang you right here," stated the gaunt old glowering range cowman, and the prisoner, who had been so quick to answer, and who had clearly been very respectful, now surprised them all when he looked old Billings squarely in the eye and said, "Mister, you do whatever you expect you got to do ... You hang me and ain't none of you going to see one red cent of that money!"

From over in the grass the JB ranch cook, a grizzled man called Jeremy, arose with an effort from one knee beside the man named Beaudry, spat amber, turned and said, "Mister Billings, this here feller is dead."

Thad walked out there. The posseman had flipped him over so that weak starshine shone across his still and greying face. Thad had never seen him before but he knew the man. "George Beaudry," he announced to the others standing around.

The other one, Zack Harmon, the tall man who had first dropped flat beside George Beaudry, also walked out there. He stood a long time gazing at the up-turned face. Then he gently wagged his head and turned slightly as he felt around for his makings. He lit up, snapped the match and with a trace of bitterness glanced around at the tough, weathered faces on all sides of him.

"He just didn't want to end his life settin' on some damned whittlers' bench out front of a lousy livery-barn hopin' someone would hire him to sweep out their saloon ... The same damned future all us rangeriders got to look forward to."

Jeremy, whose vinegary expression rarely changed, listened, looked at tall Zack Harmon, and in a surprisingly mild voice said, "I understand that. Better'n the rest of you, I expect. But mister, this ain't the answer—robbin' and stealing."

Billings turned his back and walked away. Thad sent Al Trent to help Billings catch those loose saddle animals. He took Haines and a JB rider with him.

Two other JB men volunteered to walk back and bring up their horses. Thad was agreeable and after they had departed, the other men drifted over where the mounted saddlery and camp gear were. Someone leaned to pitch in the last few twigs lying nearby and make the little fire flare up and sputter. It was getting cold, which meant the night was well advanced.

Thad turned towards his prisoner and asked a blunt question. "Where is the money?"

Harmon, with reaction setting in and with two of his trail-riding friends dead in the grass nearby, simply pointed to a pair of dangling army-style saddlebags. Thad herded him over there, took the bags down from their hanging place, opened one, saw the greenbacks, rebuckled the flap and considered the prisoner, who was also watching him.

"I guess it's too bad you fellers didn't light out yesterday," Mercer told Harmon.

The surviving outlaw turned slightly to watch old Billings and several other men bringing back the horses. "Matt wanted to. He was after us to haul out of here, divvy the money and meet again in the spring so's we could go back to raiding. ... George and I figured we needed that general store, first." Harmon faced Thad. "Well; Matt was right and a hell of a lot of good it did him, eh?"

It took the possemen an hour to get all the horses rigged out, including those animals which had belonged to the outlaws. When they finally headed down out of the little rip-gut meadow two of them were tied belly-down, arms dangling on one side, booted feet dangling on the other side.

John Billings had lost his sulphurous mood. Some of the other men, other rangemen, spoke a little from time to time with Zack Harmon, and he responded as though he and they were no different, which in most ways they weren't, but old Billings who might listen and seem to agree now and then, would not say a word to Harmon.

Al Trent rode near the rear of the posse, Norman Haines at his side. Jeremy the JB *cosinero* was back there too, and since he had spotted Haines as a gunsel right from the start, he was now giving Haines a thumbnail history of the Almarjal cow-country, along with its *mores* and range-rules. Al rode along looking pained but Norman Haines politely listened.

It was a long way back. Longer by quite a bit than it had been going out there. The reason was that they walked their horses all the way back.

It was close to dawn before they had town in sight, and by the time they went scuffing down the dusty wide main roadway, it *was* dawn. But only a few people were abroad. Walter Winters and his clerk were out front of the store, one sweeping, the other sprinkling water to the centre of the road to hold down dust at least for a few hours. They both straightened up to stare as the cavalcade passed.

At the liverybarn, where Thad turned in, the dayman was just coming to work and the nighthawk had not yet departed. They both pitched in to silently work with the possemen at off-saddling and caring for a lot of tired horses. The loose-stock was corralled out back and Thad took his prisoner, and those old army-style saddlebags, up to his office. He locked Harmon in a cell, shoved back his hat, fired up the wood-stove, then closed the roadside door and began counting the money over at his desk.

He was still doing it when old Billings came along, barged in, and remained silent until the counting was done, then he said, "All there?"

It was, so Thad nodded as he began to methodically put the money back into the saddlebags. "All here. And when I've cleared it with the circuit-ridin' judge, who is due in here the next day or two, Mister Billings, I'll bring you out your share." He took the saddlebags to an iron safe in a dark corner, pitched them in, shoved the door closed, spun the dial and turned to say, "I'm obliged for your help last night. You and your men."

Old Billings evidently took this as a signal of dismissal because he went over to the door as he said, "You're plumb welcome. Any time you need riders, let me know ..." He looked at the floor for a moment. "I got to tell you, Marshal ... you're one hell of a good lawman." He yanked open the door. "See you in a day or two," he growled, and walked out closing the door after himself.

Thad Mercer was still smiling to himself when the

gunsmith and the newcomer, Norman Haines, came along. Thad was over at the stove poking up his fire and trying to warm up some coffee.

Trent jerked a thumb over his shoulder in the direction of the roadway when he said, "Walt Winters almost danced a jig when they told him you got back the money."

Haines sat down and looked tired. "Good way to get to meet a man's neighbours," he said dryly, almost smiling in Thad's direction.

Mercer returned to the desk to also be seated. "Just so's you folks don't form a wrong opinion of the area and decide to leave," he said.

Haines continued to dryly smile, he cocked his head slightly in a quizzical manner as he continued to stare at the lawman. "We'll stay," he said quietly.

The gunsmith cleared his throat, threw them both a little hand-salute, and departed. As soon as the door had closed behind him Haines said, "Marshal; my sister and I'd admire for you to have supper with us this evening, if you'd care to."

Thad would indeed 'care' to. "I'm right obliged for the invitation," he replied, arising from behind the desk. "It'll be a pleasure."

And it would indeed be a pleasure, and if there was any way for a man to end a day which had started out with death and gunfire, so that the bad parts would be mitigated, this had to be the proper way—having supper across the table from the most handsome woman he had ever seen!